TALES TOLD AT MIDNIGHT
ALONG THE RIO GRANDE

*To
Alejandra Lara —
Enjoy!
October, 2007*

TALES TOLD AT MIDNIGHT
Along the Rio Grande

Valley Byliners
Edited by Mona Sizer

Marianna Nelson
Judy Stevens
Mona Sizer
Susan Tarrant

iUniverse, Inc.
New York Lincoln Shanghai

TALES TOLD AT MIDNIGHT Along the Rio Grande

Copyright © 2006 by Valley Byliners

All rights reserved. No part of this book may be used or reproduced by any means, graphic, electronic, or mechanical, including photocopying, recording, taping or by any information storage retrieval system without the written permission of the publisher except in the case of brief quotations embodied in critical articles and reviews.

iUniverse books may be ordered through booksellers or by contacting:

iUniverse
2021 Pine Lake Road, Suite 100
Lincoln, NE 68512
www.iuniverse.com
1-800-Authors (1-800-288-4677)

This is a work of fiction. All of the characters, names, incidents, organizations, and dialogue in this novel are either the products of the author's imagination or are used fictitiously.

ISBN-13: 978-0-595-42063-6 (pbk)
ISBN-13: 978-0-595-86408-9 (ebk)
ISBN-10: 0-595-42063-X (pbk)
ISBN-10: 0-595-86408-2 (ebk)

Printed in the United States of America

Contents

About the Valley Byliners vii

Authors ix

Part I: Whispers from the Past

The Headless Horseman of the Wild Horse Desert (Verne
    Wheelwright) 3

Margarita's Journey (Bertha Zúñiga Campos) 9

The Hello Girl (Mona D. Sizer) 13

Los Cuentos de Tio Nieves (Hernán Moreno-Hinojosa) 21
    El Rinche *21*
    The Woman in White *25*
    The Forbidden Journal *29*

Rangerville Night (Janet R. Wilder) 37

Murder at the Santa Margarita Crossroads (Mona D. Sizer) 39

Viper's Revenge (Verne Wheelwright) 45

The Devil's Gold (Sandra Vela) 49

Quinta Mazatlan (Marge Johnson) 57

Frank's Troops (Judy Stevens) 63

El Cantar de Pancho Villa (Robin Cate) 67

Part II: Crossing Over

The Quail and the Messerschmitt (Hernán Moreno-Hinojosa) 73
Literary Night at the Lopez Bar (Mona D. Sizer) 87
Personal Ghosts (Bertha Zúñiga Campos) 95
Shift Change (Judy Stevens) 101
In the Museum (Janet R. Wilder) 107
Echoes of Palo Alto (Nelly Venselaar) 113
The Hanging Room (Ann Greenfield) 115

Part III: Restless Spirits

One Hot Night in South Texas (Janice Workman) 125
El Dia de los Muertos (Robin Cate) 129
The House Who Couldn't Let Go (Eileen Mattei) 131
The Ghost Dialed 911 (Mona D. Sizer) 135
How Grandpa Got Weird (C. Dean Andersson) 147
Curandera (Georgia Tuxbury) 153
Irving (Eunice Greenhaus) 161
The House that Elrod Built (Nina Romberg) 163
Who (Eunice Greenhaus) 171
A Bruja's Benediction (Bidgie Weber) 173
Mr. Walker (Marianna Nelson) 179
Mythical Magic Valley (Nelly Venselaar) 187
Night Shift (Janice Workman) 189
The Afternoon Walk (Verne Wheelwright) 191

About the Authors 195

About the Valley Byliners

Valley Byliners was established in 1943 by a group of writers who wanted to improve their skills and enjoy fellowship with other writers. Throughout the years, the group has sponsored many writers' workshops, conferences, and writing contests.

In the 1970's and early 1980's, they published a trilogy of books on Valley history that received wide acclaim. In *Gift of the Rio*, the first in the trilogy published in 1976, the authors sought to answer the questions about the *place*, the ecology, the soil—all gifts of the Rio Grande. *Roots by the River,* published in 1978, told about some of the area's pioneers, as did *Rio Grande Roundup,* which followed in 1980. Strong threads interwoven through the three books reflect the merging cultures of the peoples on both sides of the Rio Grande.

When considering what kind of book members might write today, it was acknowledged that the area's history has been thoroughly recorded in the many good books already published. However, few of those writers had delved into the culture of legends and tales of the supernatural spun by the people. To take advantage of this rich lore, members have come together to create *Tales Told at Midnight along the Rio Grande,* which we hope you will enjoy.

Current Byliners include published and unpublished writers who love to write and are interested in learning how to improve and market their writing. Members meet monthly on the second Saturday at 1:30 p.m., usually at the Harlingen Public Library. They enjoy diverse monthly programs, inspiring workshops, and encouragement for writers in all genres. New members and visitors are always welcome.

Marjorie Johnson
Member since 1960

Authors

C. Dean Andersson
Robin Cate
Ann Greenfield
Eunice Greenhaus
Marjorie (Marge) Johnson
Eileen Mattei
Hernán Moreno-Hinojosa
Marianna Nelson
Nina Romberg
Mona D. Sizer
Judy Stevens
Georgia Tuxbury
Sandra Vela
Bidgie Weber
Verne Wheelwright
Janet R. Wilder
Janice Workman
Berta Zúñiga Campos

Acknowledgements

New Valley Byliners members are usually surprised and impressed when they learn that the 63-year-old group published three well-received books between 1975 and 1980. That example has been the 900-pound gorilla in the corner as long as I have been with Valley Byliners.

One year ago, when members began agreeing it was time for the group to publish another book, Mona Sizer stepped forward to shepherd the project as Editor-in-chief. Tales Told at Midnight along the Rio Grande exists only because of her leadership, her guidance, her encouragement, and her enthusiasm.

Mona taught workshops for us on how to write, how to develop characters, atmosphere and suspense. She motivated us and then challenged us to go home and write. She researched the self-publishing houses for us. For months she inspired, cajoled, and pestered us to write our tales of secrets and mysteries. After reading each piece, she returned it to the author with editorial suggestions about building tension, honing dialog, writing a more professional story. "Each writer is entitled to be edited," she told us, as she shaped us into better writers.

Sincerest thanks are due to our writers who proved they could stretch themselves into new genres and styles, take editing advice to heart, and produce polished stories and poems well worth reading.

Special thanks are also due to Marjorie Johnson, who contributed to the first Byliners books and this one, for keeping the Valley Byliners' name alive with the help of Adrienne Ostman for several years; and Jeff Harris, who volunteered for the laborious task of putting all the book's stories into a unified publishable format.

Eileen Mattei
President, 1996-2006

Part I

Whispers from the Past

THE HEADLESS HORSEMAN OF THE WILD HORSE DESERT

by Verne Wheelwright

A number of stories or legends are told about headless apparitions that haunt various parts of Texas, but the Headless Horseman of the Wild Horse Desert in South Texas is the one frightening legend who actually existed, was seen by reliable, sober witnesses and was shot repeatedly with rifles by men with reputations for marksmanship. Even Comanche hunting parties learned to avoid him after their arrows, shot true, simply disappeared as the horseman's black stallion galloped away.

Few people saw the mysterious horseman closely, but they agreed that he wore leather leggings, a buckskin jacket and a serape over his shoulder. He sat a typical Mexican saddle with a wide, flat saddle horn.

What terrified those who saw him was that the horseman's head, wearing a sombrero and a big grin, hung from the saddle horn, swinging and bouncing as the big horse ran through the sage, prickly pear and mesquite, easily keeping his distance from the curious, while creating fear among nearly everyone who saw or even heard of him. And he was seen widely, by vaqueros tending their herds, travelers wakened near their campfires at night, by cowboys searching for strays in the bright sunshine and blistering heat of the Wild Horse Desert, by Comanche raiders and by soldiers stationed at Fort Inge. No one questioned the existence of the headless horseman because too many reliable people had seen him, so there was a general fear and anticipation among those who had heard about the headless horseman.

Can you picture yourself sitting on a horse late at night, watching over a sleeping herd, then turning to see a headless rider silhouetted against a bright sky? And if the horse and rider started galloping toward you? Wouldn't that scare the very devil out of you? Try to imagine that scene. Even with your knowledge of the modern world, your own conviction that ghosts don't exist might be shaken. And the mid-nineteenth century was a time when people were aware and fearful of the supernatural—and the headless horseman was certainly not natural.

Some deaths were attributed to sightings of the horseman, with victims expiring from fright upon seeing the apparition, or for unknown reasons soon after an encounter. As stories were exchanged over the years, it was said that some of those who saw the horseman were so frightened their hair went completely white overnight.

The Wild Horse Desert in 1850 was disputed territory. After the Mexican-American war ended in 1848, Texas and the U.S. declared that the Rio Grande constituted the border between Texas and Mexico. Mexico, on the other hand, insisted that the Nueces River, which flows into the Gulf of Mexico at Corpus Christi, was the real border. This dispute left the area between the two rivers, known as the Wild Horse Desert, as a lawless no-man's-land. Although the U.S. had Army posts on the edges of this disputed area, and the Texas Rangers hunted down many of the more notorious of the outlaws, these few hundred military and lawmen were simply not enough of a force to take control of the area. The problems were complicated by the residents on both sides of the border, who justified a never-ending cycle of cross-border raids as retaliation or "gittin' even."

This was also a time of open range ranching, when ranchers could graze their herds on public lands, before the Civil War and before the huge King and Kennedy empires on the west side of the Wild Horse Desert existed. Barbed wire hadn't yet been invented, so ranches wouldn't be fenced in Texas for another forty years. Horses, cattle and other livestock were branded to identify their ownership, but for thieves and rustlers, brands were easy to change with a "running iron". These factors meant that herds of livestock were moved easily from one place to another, and ownership could be changed, or at least confused with the use of a hot branding iron. With this background, rustling of horses and cattle was common in 1850 Texas, and stolen animals by the thousands were moved long distances to cross the border near Brownsville and Matamoros.

Onto this scene rode the headless horseman in the summer of 1850, frightening Indian raiders and Mexican horse rustlers alike. Local ranchers were aware of the horseman, but appeared not much troubled by his presence, as he stayed away from buildings or settlements. He was seen frequently, most often at night and usually by men watching over their animals, whether cattle, sheep or horses on the open range, away from buildings and small towns. Sometimes he was seen sitting quietly erect on the large black stallion as though watching through the darkness, but more often he galloped by into the night, with no sound but the hoof beats of the large stallion. The sight of the headless man was terrifying, and as word of the sightings spread he became known among the vaqueros as "El Muerto" which the Texans translated as either "the man of death" or "death."

According to some writers, "Headless horseman sightings still occur frequently in Texas, and most are thought to be appearances of the famous El Muerto." (Treat, et al. 2005 p.53). Over the years, the legend of El Muerto has inspired books, movies and many short stories in books and on web sites. Yet, there is no suggestion that this horseman ever harmed, cursed or threatened anyone. He simply appeared, never spoke, and by his very appearance frightened people, particularly the superstitious or those with a sense of guilt.

Who was he? The story of how the headless horseman of the Wild Horse Desert came to be is nearly as fearsome as the sighting of the apparition itself.

Texas folklorist J. Frank Dobie (1955) related the historic tale of the headless horseman in his book <u>Tales of Old-time Texas</u>, and several other writers have documented the events as well. All agree that these events unfolded during the summer of 1850, and began when former Lieutenant Vidal of the Mexican army, a deserter and later an informant to the rebelling Texans, stole strings of horses from several Texas ranches, including from the ranch of Creed Taylor, a Texas Ranger and later a historic figure in Texas. Although many of the ranchers along the Nueces were away from the area dealing with a series of Comanche raids, to Vidal's misfortune Taylor was at home, and he set out quickly with a neighboring rancher, Flores, to track the stolen horses. As they trailed the bandits and their recently acquired band of horses along the Nueces River, they encountered another Texas Ranger, "Bigfoot" Wallace, who enthusiastically joined the search.

Vidal was not an amateur or accidental horse thief. He had used his good reputation, which he had earned helping the Texans during the war with Mexico, to defray suspicion from himself while he built a successful network of rustlers and horse thieves that moved their livestock into Mexico. By 1850 he was a well-known outlaw with a price on his head. But he was smart and careful, and had not yet been caught.

The ranchers and rangers tracked their horses up the Nueces River toward present day Uvalde and the former site of Fort Inge. On the Leona River about twelve miles south of Fort Inge near a mesquite and prickly pear thicket; the trackers found and ambushed the campsite of the horse thieves. Surprised while sleeping, Vidal and his band were killed quickly. Wallace suggested that instead of taking Vidal back for the reward, they send a warning to all thieves, rustlers and raiders in the vicinity. With the agreement of the others, Wallace set to work.

He picked a large, black, mustang stallion from the stolen herd. The horse was wild and fearful of humans, but was roped, blindfolded with a red bandana, hobbled and saddled. Wallace then beheaded Vidal's corpse, set the body in the saddle, tied the hands to the pommel and the feet to the stirrups, then tied the stirrups together under the quivering horse's belly. With rawhide, the body was tied securely into an upright position. A piece of rawhide was stretched through Vidal's mouth, forcing it into a wide grin. The head was tied securely to his sombrero, which in turn was tied to the large flat saddle horn. With the rider and his head firmly in their places, the horse was untied and the blindfold removed. The frightened stallion did everything he could to rid himself of his foul smelling burden, but without success. At last, he galloped off into the desert, and Texas legend. All present agreed not to reveal what had happened to Vidal, hoping that the sight of the headless horsemen would frighten superstitious Indians and horse thieves from the area.

It is said that the stallion tried to rejoin wild mustang herds, but the other horses were terrified by the figure on the stallion's back, and fled in panic. Thus the horseman was seen, apparently herding large numbers of mustangs as they raced across the desert. But the stallion and his rider were usually seen alone, rejected by the other wild horses, yet fearful of men, horse and horsemen were united in solitude. Docia Williams (1955) described the black horse as "Wild to start with, afraid of men, and now living with the stench of a decaying corpse on his back, the mustang carried his burden far from civilized areas."

Wallace's apparition was apparently effective, because the sightings and the rumors spread across south Texas quickly, and the legend remains today. The actual horseman continued to ride the Wild Horse Desert for some years, although the record is not clear how many. Eventually, several men working together managed to track the black stallion and capture him, cutting off the big saddle and the mummified rider. The buckskin jacket and corpse held several bullet holes, arrows and even Indian spears. Vidal's dried remains were buried in a small cemetery on the La Trinidad ranch near the small community of Ben Bolt, just south of Alice, Texas. Taylor and Wallace eventually acknowledged the events, and the tale is recounted in Wallace's memoir. But the sightings of the headless horseman of the Wild Horse Desert continued.

With the construction of well-lighted freeways reports of the horseman have decreased considerably, but if you happen to travel the country roads in South Texas at night, watch for a black horse running nearby whose rider at first looks unusual—until you realize that his sombrero topped head is hanging from his saddle horn. Your adventure will then become the most recent sighting of the headless horseman of the Wild Horse Desert.

MARGARITA'S JOURNEY

by Bertha Zúñiga Campos

A tired group of travelers arrived at the banks of the Rio Grande in the summer of 1918. The travelers from Cerralvo, Nuevo Leon, in northeastern Mexico, arrived exhausted from the 60-mile wagon ride. It was still dark, in those early hours before dawn. When time hangs suspended between present and past, the future looms uncertain and frightening on the other side. The travelers made their way cautiously through the tall grasses that grow along the banks of the river. Every now and then, they crouched low and hid where the river curved around the bank. They watched the river closely for signs of activity on the water, any waves or ripples or sounds that would warn of an approaching boat. They had been warned about men in boats, patrolling.

These were the perilous times of the Bandit Wars along the Rio Grande Valley on the river that borders Texas and Mexico. Mexican rebel Pancho Villa, resentful of U.S. involvement in Mexican politics and business interests, made a pastime of raiding farms and robbing trains along the border.

To quell settlers' fears, the Texas governor sent the National Guard and the newly formed Texas Rangers to secure the border. The only problem was that these men often did not differentiate between the bandits and Mexican Americans who maintained ties to family across the river. More often than not, the lawmen would shoot first and ask questions later.

The travelers from Cerralvo had good reason to be afraid. One of them was a little girl, five years old. She is my mother. She has told her story so often through the years that I hear it in my dreams. It is a sad story, interspersed with tender moments. It is special because it defines who we are as a family. She tells it because it helps her to make sense of her life, and sad as it is, I hear it because I would not be here were it not for her.

The waters of the Rio Grande looked dark and menacing to five-year-old Margarita Viviana Salinas. She wrapped her arms around the man who lifted her on the raft that would carry her across.

"*Sientate aquí.* Sit here, niña," he said. "We will soon be on the other side and then you can go with your mother."

Margarita shut her eyes. She wasn't going to let herself be scared. Her feet were touching the cold waters of the river. Though the current was calm, its faint gurgling noises belied the myriad horrors that she imagined lay beneath. To the child's mind, the tangled weed beneath the surface became water snakes and biting fish. Weeds with razor edges felt like bony fingers pulling at her, to drown her. She began to pray a child's prayer: "*Por favor, Diosito, no me dejes tener miedo.*" "Please, God, don't let me be afraid."

Her mother swam beside her, silent. Maybe she too is scared, Margarita thought, though she would rather believe her mother was not afraid of anything.

Margarita tried putting her mind on other things, but she was cold and tired, and hungry. She could not remember the last time she had eaten. She wondered if her father was looking for her. What had gone through his mind when he realized she was gone?

She was too young to understand why her mother had taken her so abruptly from her father's house, but she sensed that it was serious enough for this ordeal. She feared she would never see her father again. How much does any child understand about the ways of adults when she is just five? What does any child know of politics, family feuds, social standing?

Pancho Villa's raids had destroyed much of the Salinas family holdings, leaving Margarita's father wealthier on paper than in actual property. In the town of Cerralvo, a story circulated that Villa had a vendetta against the Salinas family because one of the daughters had married a gringo who had faked a gun sale to Villa. But who knew if that were true or not?

The truth was that Eduardo Salinas's timing had not been good. During the revolution he had estranged himself from his wife, Margarita's mother, a woman many years younger than he, and he had used family connections to take custody of their child. Now landless and destitute, he had to leave Margarita in the care of his family while he tried to make a living off the mines around Cerralvo. Margarita would not understand all that was happening until many years later. For now, though one revolution had ended, another personal one embroiled her in its midst.

Drifting on the river, she tried to make sense of the events of the previous day when she had left Cerralvo. Margarita remembered her mother casting anxious looks around her as she came to the front door of the Salinas house. Margarita had thrown the door open and run to her mother, despite the angry protests of her caregiver.

"Mamá!" she had cried. She knew her mother was unwelcome in the house.

Kneeling, her mother met Margarita's eyes. "Shh," she whispered. "Tell your aunt that we are going to see your grandfather, and we will be back before your father returns from the mines."

And so they had left her father's house. Out of the courtyard, they broke into a run. A chilly wind moved the branches of the *sabinales*, the ancient grove of trees of Cerralvo. It sent shivers through Margarita's body as she ran. They ran without stopping, her mother's hand squeezing hers so tightly that it hurt.

When they reached the cemetery at the entrance of the town, Margarita's mother suddenly fainted from exhaustion. Margarita screamed, throwing herself over her mother's limp body.

"*Mamá! Levantate, Mamá!* Get up! Get up!" she screamed. "Please mamá, don't die."

Then strong arms pried her away from her mother and carried her to a mule cart that waited nearby. The strangers, a man and woman, brought her mother next and laid her in the cart, pulling a tarp over them both. They began their journey to the river. With each jolt of the wagon, Margarita wondered if she would ever see her father again. She wondered where she was going and what the next day would bring. She closed her eyes more to forget the past than to avoid the water.

"*Ya cruzamos, Mage.*" The harsh-sounding word was her mother's nickname for her. She preferred the sound of Margarita, especially when *"Mi Tesoro,* my treasure," her father's nickname for her, followed it.

When she opened her eyes, the sight of the water lilies on the northern bank of the Rio Grande pulled Margarita back to the present. The group had crossed the river safely. Lifting her off the raft, the stranger ordered her to grab hold of the tall grasses and pull herself onto the riverbank. Finally she sat with her mother, and they both looked towards the east. It was daybreak. The sun was low in the horizon. Soon it would burn off the dew on the ground, but for now, the crisp morning air invigorated Margarita, filling her with hope.

"Thank you, God," she whispered.

The immigrants who cross the Rio Grande attempting to reach the United States each have their own perilous story of survival and a compelling reason to get to "el otro lado" the other side. The haggard ones who succeed in crossing are looking for a better life. Like Margarita, many find their version of happiness. Others do not. The immigrant's journey has gone on for generations, and despite rivers, deserts, and mountains, it continues today.

THE HELLO GIRL

by Mona D. Sizer

Dim light leaked from the speedometer circle on the dashboard. It spilled onto the brake, clutch, and accelerator pedals sticking up from the rubber mat under her feet. Beyond the headlights was only formless darkness. No stars, no moon. The heavy bank of clouds rolling in with the morning's wet norther had blotted them out.

Anna Bevens shivered and shrugged her shoulders to ease the strain. So long as she'd been on the narrow concrete strip of farm-to-market road, driving had been fairly easy. At the turnoff to Cragg's ranch, the caliche had melted away and the road had turned into a slick pair of ruts.

Driving in second gear at ten miles an hour, she steered around the low places filled with standing water. Her arms ached from manhandling the steering wheel, but she didn't dare let the car come to a stop that would mire it permanently in the delta mud.

At the same time, she worried what she would do if she had to change a flat.

She had a patch kit. She had a flashlight. She'd fixed a flat before. But never in mud. Never in the dark. She shivered again, dreading the thought of getting out in the icy, windy darkness.

Another half mile and the salt cedar brake ended. The wind hit her broadside. The car fishtailed violently almost jerking the wheel out of her hands. The rear wheels dropped into the crossing ruts from the side road and the car slewed sideways.

Lord! The road was a swamp. How much farther was this ranch house?

Just as she was turning the car around in the crossroad, her headlights picked out a shape. A horseman in a pale slicker, his hat pulled low over his face, galloped straight toward her. Gritting her teeth, she stamped on the brake and clutch simultaneously. Her right hand dropped to her purse stuffed between the bucket seats. Only when he pulled his horse to a sliding halt, did she realize he was on the other side of a barbed-wire fence.

A second rider appeared behind him, loping out of the dark. She was sure both were armed and dangerous. She shivered. Resolutely, she shifted into low gear and held her breath. The wheels spun, but miraculously the car lurched upward out of the ruts. She shifted into second to get back to ten miles an hour. On her left she could make out the horsemen. They seemed to be escorting her. Just so long as they stayed on the other side of the fence.

Anna's hand slipped back to her purse. In the bottom beneath the night letter and her coin purse and wallet with the pictures of her mother and her daughter was the one thing her cheating, abusive husband had left her, the one thing she would carry with her for the rest of her life.

She had made up her mind if any man came too near her car at night, she'd use the nickel-plated Colt .22. In Texas's Lower Rio Grande Valley in 1940 a woman couldn't be too careful. It was still bandit country. And bandits could be anybody.

At last she glimpsed a light—small, yellow, too low-hanging to be a star. She breathed a sigh of relief dampened by the message she'd written in her own hand on yellow Western Union paper.

No one would be glad to read what she had brought. She just hoped they'd have a cup of hot coffee for the messenger.

The Valley wasn't Anna's choice. The primitive, isolated delta formed by the Rio Grande in the southern-most tip of Texas wasn't where she had expected to live her adult life and rear her child.

But plans change. In just three short years, her family had gone from bright hope to tragic loss. First, her father had died suddenly. Then she'd been forced to divorce her husband. To escape him completely, she'd fled from all she knew, all she loved, taking her mother and six-year-old daughter with her.

Into a half-wild land, they went—three gently-bred women to live alone on a farmstead seven miles from a small country town. Fortunately, they weren't totally impoverished. Anna hadn't had to chop weeds in a cotton field or drive a tractor. No one would have expected her to do that. Like a country gentlewoman, she'd put the quarter section into the hands of a reputable farmer.

But cotton and grain payments came only when the crop was in. Between the payments, which might be small depending on the weather, they might run out of money. She had to find a job.

In an understated dress bought nearly ten years before at Marshall Field's in Chicago, she confidently applied to be a teacher. The gray-haired, hatchet-faced female principal in her sensible "nurses" Oxfords didn't even offer her a chair. My mother was divorced. She need not bother to apply.

To her horror she discovered that rumors had spread about her. Divorced. Shame. As if the mere presence of a woman so undutiful to her husband might contaminate the innocent children, the principal wouldn't consider her. Even her education in speech arts from Galloway College, with professional studies in Chicago, Atlanta, and Dallas was worth nothing.

Until the crops were harvested, they had absolutely no money to spend on anything except food and gasoline. She couldn't even send her daughter to Sunday school because Ellen had outgrown her shoes. They had no money to buy a new pair of patent leathers. Her daughter was wearing twenty-five-cent *huaraches* from Mexico.

Anna was on the verge of writing a pleading letter to her ex-husband when she heard of a job, one that no decent woman wanted. The growing town needed a girl in the evening at the telephone exchange.

Her mother was shocked. She folded her arms and shook her head. No daughter of hers was going to work as a telephone operator.

"We have to eat," Anna said. "And my daughter doesn't have any clothes for school."

Her mother's eyes filled with tears. She hugged her arms tight across her mutilated chest. The utter hopelessness of a woman whose body had been slashed and stitched, then burned with radiation to prevent a recurrence of cancer, a woman whose dearly beloved husband had died suddenly at Christmas, a woman who'd had the best life had to offer now reduced to genteel poverty.

"They'll pay me for honest work, Mother," Anna pleaded. "I promise I won't do anything bad."

"But your reputation—"

"Mother, it's already gone."

"That Fred—" Her mother put her hand over mouth to stop words she'd never uttered in her life.

"He's gone too. And good riddance."

Her mother's hand dropped. She hugged her body again, absolutely speechless with shame because they had no choice. "You know what they call them? Those girls that work—there?"

Her daughter shrugged, but her mouth trembled. "Yes. They're Hello Girls."

Telephone operators answered the rings of their customers by saying "Hello." The reputation of the "Hello Girls" was a step below single girls, who worked in shops where strange men asked to be waited on. At least, those girls were out in public where others could see and monitor their behavior.

Telephone operators were much worse than that. They were definitely fast and loose. After all, they said "Hello" to strange men to whom they had not been properly introduced. And who knew what they might say on those private lines where nobody could listen in?

Since many more men than women made calls, men would flirt with the girls, call them sweet names, beg for dates after work. Then whether the girl went out with them or not, they bragged or lied to other men about what a "hot time" they'd had.

Their stories were corroborated by people with party lines who saw nothing wrong with "listening in." Some of them delighted in reporting all sorts of indecent propositions and assignations. In the minds of most solid citizens, the telephone and the girls who operated it had brought about a degradation of civilized society.

Without a choice Anna went to work in the most scandalous position of all. She was the evening girl. Who knew who she might meet after work and what she might do? Moreover, she had volunteered to carry night letters—telegrams that came in to the switchboard for people who had no telephones. Since someone who could drive a car was required, my mother was happy to do it for an extra dollar each. A dollar was ten hours' pay for her.

Of course, her driving around the county had come to the attention of the county. Sheriff Howard Cragg patrolled regularly and knew everybody who traveled the roads at night.

The sheriff himself opened the door of the ranch house. His eyes narrowed, and his mouth twisted in a sneer. "Hey! Well, lookee who's here. The Hello Girl."

My mother knew him too, and she didn't like him. He'd harassed her on three separate occasions. Once over the telephone, and twice in the grocery store where he'd followed her when she came in to buy a nickel loaf of white bread and a dime jar of Kraft pimiento cheese.

Once he'd made her pull her car over into the barditch and had lectured her about her reputation and how the town didn't need women with "no daddies for their brats." He'd even suggested that she was "driving around the county at night meeting men."

Now, rather than let her into his warm bright house, he started to close the door, but my mother hadn't driven all that distance to retreat without delivering her message. She raised the yellow envelope in the porch light. "I'm delivering a night letter to Ruth Mix."

He reached for it. "I'll see that she gets it."

My mother took a backward step. "It's for Ruth Mix."

"I'm her husband." He scowled. His voice grated. "You give it here. I'll deliver it. You get on off."

"That's not according to rules and regulations."

"Who is it, Howard?"

He looked straight into Anna's eyes and smirked. "Nobody important."

Stung, she raised her voice. "I have a telegram, Miss Mix!"

"A telegram?"

Cowboy boot heels rang across the hardwood floors. Pretty and blonde, but definitely past her prime, Ruth pushed her husband out of the way with an exasperated smile. "Come in, for goodness sake. Howard, what have you got for manners? Leaving a woman standing in the rain and cold?"

Gratefully, Anna stepped inside. She drew a deep breath. "Miss Mix."

The woman waited expectantly—a smile on her face.

"I have a night letter."

"From Daddy?" Not waiting for any answer, she turned to Howard and slapped her hands together in triumph. "The deal must've gone through. We'll be out of this place and back in Hollywood before you know it."

While the sheriff's scowl blackened at the prospect, my mother closed her eyes. The paper crumpled a little as she clutched it. Then silently, she passed it over.

"For God's sake, Howard! Don't stand there like a cigar store Indian. Go get her a cup of coffee." Ruth Mix tore the telegram open.

Anna's eyes met the sheriff's. A silent message passed between them.

"Oh, no. Oh, no!" Ruth put out her hand. Her husband caught it and tried to draw her in against his chest.

Under the date October 12, 1940, my mother had brought the message that cowboy movie star Tom Mix had been roaring west in his famous custom-built

Cord Roadster with the set of longhorns on the radiator. It had gone off the road and turned over near Phoenix, Arizona. He'd died instantly.

Then a strange thing happened. The shattered woman needed more than a gruff, rude man to hold her in her grief. Instead of reaching for her husband, Ruth Mix reached out for Anna. Like sisters they embraced each other offering comfort for fathers lost forever. They both wept.

The sheriff guided them to sit on the cowhide sofa and left to bring them coffee. He'd laced his wife's with whiskey.

At last, when Ruth had cried herself out, my mother rose to go. Sheriff Cragg picked up her purse. His eyebrows rose as he hefted it. Before he handed it to her, he slipped his hand underneath. He flexed his fingers and slid his palm along the bottom where he could feel every shape in the soft black leather.

Angry and frightened, Anna snatched it from him.

His eyes narrowed as he looked her up and down as if seeing her for the first time. She settled the strap of her purse firmly over her shoulder, lifted her chin in her proud way that asked no favors, and walked out.

He followed her out onto the porch and closed the door behind him. "You keep that gun in your purse if you know what's good for you. Don't be takin' potshots at my riders."

On the porch she faltered. The two riders in yellow slickers sat their horses by her car. Cold rain dripped from their hat brims pulled low over their faces. They were menacing as villains in a Western movie. One's mount blocked her door.

But she'd be damned if she'd let him keep her shivering in the rain while he lectured her. She slid her right hand into her purse and closed it over the little .22. She didn't draw it. Instead, she looked directly at the sheriff. "So long as they stay on their horses, they can ride wherever they want."

With that she stepped down off the porch. One step, two. She was prepared to duck under the horse's neck to get to the car door when the rider reined his animal backward.

She pulled open the door. Before she climbed in, she looked back at Cragg. "If any man comes within arm's length of my car door, I'll shoot. Just remember that, and put out the word. I'm doing honest work delivering telegrams like the one your wife got tonight. I'm not out riding around for any other reason. Not now. Not ever."

He grunted.

She climbed into her car and slammed the door.

His expression murderous, he stepped down from the porch and reached for the door handle. Before he could open it, she pulled the Colt. Its nickel-plate barrel flashed in the light spill from the porch. She didn't warn, didn't challenge, didn't even speak.

He stared down at the gun and then into her face. Carefully, slowly, he withdrew his hand and stepped back. Not turning his back on her, he retreated to the porch. She turned the key in the ignition, switched on the headlights, and drove away into the wet darkness.

She was frighteningly late getting home that night. Her mother had waited up, frantic with worry, for though she worked at the telephone company, we couldn't afford a phone way out in the country. The older woman had hot soup and chocolate and had filled a hot water bottle for her daughter's bed.

After Anna tucked herself in, she couldn't sleep for thinking about what had happened. She wondered what the sheriff would do now that she had drawn a gun on him. The weapon itself wasn't illegal, but her drawing down on the law most certainly was. He could easily take it away from her if he wanted to. For weeks she waited for a visit. Gradually, she relaxed, but she never forgot what happened that night.

Shortly thereafter, Ruth Mix left for California and never returned.

A nice ending to the story would be that the sheriff and Anna became fast friends. But that's not the way the story ended.

The sheriff was always rude and gruff although he never harassed her again. He knew a woman armed with a Colt .22 could be just as dangerous as a man at close range. My mother tucked her purse under her arm and stayed out of his way.

Spitefully, he never bothered to correct the impression that she was fast and loose. Innocent though she was, to most of the town's upstanding citizens, for as long as she lived, she remained the Hello Girl.

Though she carried her gun till the day she died, to my knowledge she never actually had to shoot anyone.

At least she never told *me* that she did.

Los Cuentos de Tio Nieves

EL RINCHE

by Hernán Moreno-Hinojosa

The most important establishment in Mier, on the Mexican side of *el Valle del Rio Grande*, was *la Cantina del Camino Real*. For many years it served as social center for this small community doubling as local post office where Agapo, the bartender, would find himself serving not only *cerveza*—beer but dispensing mail as well. The cantina also served the community well as town hall where once a week the mayor, *Don* Ruben Ramos de la Rosa, would preside over the public meetings. Don Ruben always began his town hall meetings by bragging about his beautiful young wife, and then he would apprise the men of the goings-on of the previous week. He would report on the progress of the ongoing *guerillas*—skirmishes that plagued Mexico during those days and he provided intelligence on the movements of the *Villista* and *Carranzista* troops. Wrong or right his intelligence came directly from the newspaper over in Reynosa. None-the-less, with most of the laypeople unable or unwilling to read, the town hall meetings were always deemed a complete success.

This arrangement suited the men well as women were not permitted in the cantina and the men could discuss matters of utmost urgency without the meddling or interference of those of the fairer sex. During this era *Tío* Nieves Hinojosa resided in Mier and worked on the Texas side of the border.

Tío Nieves, a young and carefree soul in those day, arrived on horseback from Texas and proceeded to the Cantina del Camino Real. Outside the cantina

Nieves handed his gray horse over to one of the local boys, "*Chamaco*—boy, take my horse over to the stable, please. Here are twenty *centavos* for your trouble."

The boy's face erupted into a smile. The small, shiny silver twenty-centavo Mexican coin was a lot of money for the young boy. "*Si*, Tío Nieves, your horse is in good hands!"

Nieves strolled into the cantina, "Agapo, do I have any mail?"

Agapo stared at Nieves' low-slung empty leather holster, "Ah, no, Nieves, *el correo* has not come yet. If you don't mind me asking Nieves, where is your *pistola*?"

Nieves half turned and stared down at his empty holster, "I had a run-in with a *rinche* on the Texas side."

"*Los* rinches!" Agapo's face was wide with concern.

"One rinche, Agapo. Old Captain Bill and don't worry, he didn't get the tequila." Nieves reached into his left shirt pocket and handed Agapo fifty American dollars. "Here is your forty percent, Agapo."

Agapo quickly counted the money. "That crazy old rinche finally made captain? That old reprobate thinks he speaks good Spanish because he ends every word with an 'o,' or an 'a,' but tell me, Nieves, what happened to your .45?"

"Give me a cerveza, Agapo, and I will tell you the story." Agapo put the money away and retrieved a cold beer, opened the bottle and set it in front of Nieves.

Nieves took a long cool drink, gasped and wiped his mouth with his right shirtsleeve. "As you know, Agapo, I always hide the tequila in a secure place, an arroyo on the Texas side that everyone believes is haunted."

Agapo opened his eyes wide. "Haunted?"

"Si," Nieves continued, "they say they hear strange noises at night. No one will go near there at night."

"And you are not afraid?"

"No. One night I camped out in that arroyo. Around midnight the most awful racket you can imagine awakened me. *Espantos*—spooks cracking bones, rattling chains and cackling, I thought, and signed myself with the Holy Sign. So I took my Colt .45 in my hand and proceeded to investigate."

Agapo's dark eyes were wide with wonder, his black eyebrows came together above the bridge of his ponderous nose and he nervously tucked at his long left sideburn. Nieves wondered how Agapo could serve drinks all day and still manage to keep his white shirt so clean.

"What did you learn?"

Nieves indicated that Agapo should lean in closer, then looking quickly both ways Nieves whispered, "*Tejones.*"

"*¿Tejones*—raccoons? Nieves, what do you mean?"

Nieves put his index finger to his face. "Shhh, not so loud Agapo, yes, raccoons. A family of raccoons have a nest in a cave in that arroyo. They make the noise at night that frightens everyone, and that is where I hide the tequila from the Texas Rangers."

Agapo looked puzzled. "I still don't understand, Nieves, what happened to your .45?"

"Let me finish, but first, Agapo, fetch me another beer. Make sure it is cold."

*   *   *   *

As far as pistols were concerned Nieves favored the new Government Model, 1911 Colt .45 automatic pistol, to the more common revolvers of the day. The automatic pistol had its virtues. It was quicker to deploy and carried more bullets in its box magazine than the older revolver. Tío Nieves found the automatic pistol pleasant to shoot and very accurate.

"*Los avisos de la quarenta-y-cinco,*" Nieves often said, "*son bien conocidos.*" Loosely translated, "When the .45 announces its presence, its presence is quickly acknowledged." He was referring to the impressionable sound of the pistol's slide being racked to feed a bullet. That menacing sound signaled that the pistol was ready to be shot and shot until the shooter was out of bullets—a sound not disdained by the reasonable and prudent, nor taken lightly by even the bravest of men.

Tío Nieves carried his .45 in a low-slung leather holster with the hammer down on an empty chamber, the magazine fully loaded, and the safety off. Drawing the pistol and racking the slide fed a bullet into the chamber and cocked the hammer. Now the slightest touch to the trigger would cause the gun to discharge, and the shooting process could be repeated merely by pulling the trigger until the magazine was empty.

*   *   *   *

"Rinche Bill stopped me in that arroyo, Agapo, just outside the cave where I had hidden the tequila. My .45 immediately caught his eye. He did not find it unusual that I was carrying a gun. What the rinche captain wanted to know was what I was doing with an automatic Colt."

"You must have stolen this *pistola*." The rinche said in bad Spanish.

"*No señor rinche,*" I protested. "I bought it."

"It says here," the rinche pointed to the slide, "Government Model—that means that this *pistola* is property of the United States Government. *Hombre*, I can throw you in prison for that."

Of course, I knew that the captain was making an issue out of what was merely the model name of the pistol. Still, I have never been one to confuse stupidity with courage. "Is that what it says, señor rinche?" I feigned ignorance as best I could.

"Can't you read, hombre?" The captain retorted.

Grinning sheepishly I answered, "That is it, señor rinche, I never did learn how to read."

"And so the rinche captain kept your .45?"

"*Si* Agapo. I sacrificed my .45 so that the rinche would not find our tequila. I sold the tequila to the *gringos* and have enough money to buy a new .45 with some cash to spare."

"Look," Agapo said pointing toward the swinging front bar doors, "here comes the mayor for his weekly town meeting."

Nieves took long steps walking around the bar. "Agapo, the Colt truck was at the hardware store. I'm sneaking out the back way to get a new Colt before that old fool starts ranting and raving again, about how lucky he is to be married to the most beautiful woman in all of Mexico!"

"Well, Nancy *is* a real beauty. You have to give the mayor *that*."

"Yes she is, Agapo. Too bad none of her positive qualities wear off on that old fool we have for a mayor!"

Los Cuentos de Tio Nieves

THE WOMAN IN WHITE
by Hernán Moreno-Hinojosa

In those days all the men carried guns. *Tío* Nieves Hinojosa lived in Mier, a tiny town just south of the Texas/old Mexico border, on the Mexican side of *el Valle del Rio Grande*. During the recent past *Villistas* and *Carranzistas* traded shots here. The people were nervous and unsettled.

Tío Nieves heard the story circulating around town about a ghostly presence. A woman dressed all in white with a long white veil was seen at midnight, walking slowly through the municipal cemetery. She did not wail, she did not moan, but she was always seen at the stroke of midnight, the witching hour. The mystery woman walked silently between the sun-bleached tombstones and crosses that marked the final resting place of the beloved deceased of this small town. It was even reported that on more than one occasion, this ghostly woman had been seen vanishing into a mausoleum.

Tío Nieves loved a mystery and knew even then that he would be investigating the truth of the reported apparition. He knew well enough that curiosity had killed the cat and even though his friends called him *gato* because of his green eyes, this *cat* packed a pistol and would perhaps not be so easy to kill.

When Nieves returned from Texas that day, people south of the border still spoke in hushed whispers of *la mujer que se aparece de noche en el campo santo*. Was she an evil apparition, perhaps the harbinger of still more tragedy to befall this normally peaceful little community? Could she even be *La Llorona*, that most famous of Mexican apparitions? Or perhaps she was simply a lost soul whose true love had been felled by a Villista or Carranzista bullet. Now perhaps she wandered the graveyard at night seeking to be re-united in death with her lover.

At the local *cantina* Nieves bolstered his courage with a stiff drink. Tonight, at the stroke of midnight, he would know the truth!

Tío Nieves never did say how long he stayed at the cantina, nor how well into his cups he was when he ventured into the local cemetery that dark night. He did report feeling good and knowing no fear when he concealed himself in the graveyard to await the mystery woman. After all, he reminded himself, he stood on holy ground. The Holy Mother Church consecrated this graveyard. No evil thing can walk here, he reassured himself as he slumped down with his back to the nearest tombstone.

Perhaps half-an-hour later Nieves spied a flash of white moving slowly between the tombstones. *"¡Santa Madre de Dios!"* He exclaimed, nervously making the Sign of the Cross. The figure in white stopped. She must have heard him!

The mystery woman glanced briefly over her shoulder at Nieves before she hurried away.

"¡Espera!" Nieves shouted, "Wait!"

The woman in white moved away even more rapidly.

Now he found himself running after the woman in white who seemed to be heading straight into the mausoleum.

"What manner of apparition is this," Nieves asked himself under his breath, "that flees from a man of flesh-and-blood?"

It only took a moment for him to figure out that the ghostly woman must have stepped inside the mausoleum. She could not have gone anywhere else. With nervous fingers he reached for the door. The door was cold to the touch but, to his surprise, it was not locked! *Con su pistola en la mano* Nieves leaned on the door. It creaked eerily as he slowly pushed against it with his shoulder.

The interior of the mausoleum was pitch black. Nothing seemed to stir. Still, the woman could not have gone anywhere else. Nieves racked the slide on his big Colt automatic. The metallic grating sound, rude enough to wake the dead, was punctuated by a pleading woman's voice that echoed from within the tomb, *"¡No me mates Nieves—soy yo!*—Don't kill me Nieves—it is only me!" The mystery woman knew his name!

In itself that detail was not so strange. After all, Mier was a small town where everyone knew everyone else. Still, there was something unsettlingly familiar about that voice.

"Come out," Nieves demanded, "and I will not shoot." The woman had no idea that Nieves did not have a target to shoot at. Even all dressed up in white the woman was invisible cloaked in the darkness of the tomb.

"Come out into the light of the moon," he insisted, "that we may see each other face to face."

A handsome buxom woman of medium stature and ample attributes dressed all in white meekly emerged from the tomb, her big doe-eyes even larger with apprehension.

"*¡La esposa del alcade!*" Tío Nieves now found himself staring in amazement at the face of the mayor's comely, young wife!

Finding her composure the woman exclaimed, "Nieves, tell no one about this and I shall see to it that my husband rewards you well for your cooperation."

"Then your husband knows that you walk the cemetery at night?" Nieves inquired incredulously.

"Of course not." The woman scowled, squirming to keep her white shawl on her ample shoulders. "No one must know about this."

"What are you doing *here* at this hour, dressed up like La Llorona, scaring all the townspeople?"

"That," she retorted, still struggling with her shawl and her dignity, "is not for you to know."

"Doesn't your gardener Severo," Nieves inquired, pointing in the direction that the woman had come from, "live just beyond the graveyard?"

"Enough!" the woman insisted, a flush evident even in the ambient light of the moon appeared on her face, "Do you wish to be recompensed for your trouble, *sí o no?*"

"Silver can buy many things," Nieves answered, "those who pay the wages call it *the poor man's gold.*"

"Gossip," he continued philosophically, "benefits no one and is *never* becoming of men."

*   *   *   *

That night by the light of the moon, in the municipal cemetery of Mier, Tío Nieves Hinojosa chose the better of the two.

Los Cuentos de Tio Nieves

THE FORBIDDEN JOURNAL
by Hernán Moreno-Hinojosa

At the *Cantina del Camino Real*, the gathering place and post office in Mier, Agapo the bartender and unofficial postmaster was conducting mail call. "Nieves! Where is Nieves Hinojosa?"

"Nieves probably went to *el otro cachete*," one of the local men suggested, referring to the Texas side of the Valley as *the other cheek*.

"No," Agapo replied, "he was here last night and walked home around midnight."

"If he stayed until midnight, then he must be sleeping it off." Someone else murmured.

"If one of you sees him, tell him that package he's been waiting for arrived by mail this morning."

* * * *

Late that afternoon, around nightfall, Nieves stumbled into the cantina to collect his mail. "Agapo," he called, walking across the floor to the bar, "you have something for me?"

"*Sí*, Nieves." Agapo eagerly reached under the bar and handed Nieves a package wrapped in brown paper, the odd postage stamps cancelled in purple ink. "How about a 'hair of the dog that bit you, no?'" Agapo offered.

Nieves nodded as he unwrapped his package. The men were just beginning to gather for their evening drink.

"That package came to you all the way from Barcelona, Spain," Agapo excitedly stated, setting a cold beer in front of Nieves.

Nieves said nothing. Agapo, arms folded across his barrel chest, finally demanded, "Well?"

"Well, what?"

"¡Caramba, hombre! Who do you know in Barcelona?"

"He is an antiquities dealer acquaintance of mine ..."

Agapo's dark eyes opened wide. "You have been to Barcelona?"

"No, never."

Agapo threw his head back. "Nieves, you are not making any sense. How do you know someone as important as an antiquities dealer in such a faraway place and yet say you have never been to Barcelona?"

Nieves grabbed his bottle of beer and moved to the table closest to the bar. It was already dim within the cantina and so Nieves adjusted the wick on the oil lamp at his table. The soot covered glass flue brightened, casting eerie shadows all around the cantina. "*Don* Alberto, the antiquities dealer, came through here about a year ago. He was interested in purchasing Indian artifacts."

Agapo wiped his hands on a white towel. "I didn't know that you collected Indian artifacts, Nieves?"

"I don't," Nieves replied matter-of-factly, "but my great-grandfather, Jesusito Hinojosa, was a great collector of Indian artifacts. When my father died, I as the eldest son, retained his belongings."

"So you sold your great-grandfather's Indian artifacts to this antiquities dealer?"

Nieves shook his head. "No. Don Alberto was mainly interested in Indian arrowheads and during his lifetime my great-grandfather managed to collect seven authentic Apache and Comanche arrowheads. Don Alberto and Jesusito were both Spaniards and so Don Alberto was especially interested in those arrowheads collected by one of his countrymen. I gave Don Alberto four of the seven arrowheads removed from my great-grandfather's body in return for his promise to send me banned books from Spain to read."

Agapo quickly signed himself with the Holy Sign. "I know you like to read, but to *read* books banned by the Church is sacrilege!" Agapo looked ready to throw Nieves out of his cantina along with his forbidden book.

Nieves gave Agapo a bothered look. "This book was not banned by the Church. It was banned by the Spanish Crown."

"The Spanish government banned this book, not the Church?"

"Yes. This journal is authentic, penned in Indian ink by the famous Spanish cartographer, Manuel Luis María de Marquez. Here in part it reads: *Por obra y gracia de Dios, hoy me encuentro sano y salvo para dar esta revelación …*"

Agapo again made the Holy Sign, repeating what Nieves had just read, "*By the grace and will of God, today I am alive and well and able to make this revelation—* and what is the revelation, Nieves?"

Nieves shifted in his chair. "The journal itself appears to be a warning of sorts. Perhaps the Spanish government banned it, fearful that exploration of the New World would cease if the contents of this journal became common knowledge."

By this time all eyes and ears were on Nieves and the cantina became as quiet as a tomb. Nieves stood, reached into his pocket and retrieved a large Mexican silver coin. "Agapo," he said, tossing the coin across the bar, "the drinks are on me …" and he began to read the forbidden journal from the beginning:

El Valle del Rio Grande:

Manuel and Felipe are riding through their property looking for stray cattle. "I am missing one yearling heifer, Felipe; I think it may have wandered into yonder arroyo and is unable to scale the steep arroyo walls."

"You may be right, Manuel. Let us leave our horses here, and go down into the arroyo to investigate."

By trade Manuel is a cartographer. Felipe does not have a profession other than adventurer, but he is young and his brother still has hopes for him. Perhaps their joint venture of raising cattle and horses in *Terra Nova* will bear fruit and, after a few years, they shall return to Spain to find brides. The two brothers walk together to the edge of the arroyo, and then slide down the sandy ridge. Once below they follow the arroyo west.

"There was a great hurricane in the Gulf last year Felipe, the Year of our Lord, 1806." And Manuel doffs his hat and signs himself with the Holy Sign.

Felipe replies solemnly, "I remember brother. This arroyo ran like a great river, filled to the brim with raging water. Where do you suppose all that water went? Do you know, brother, if arroyos run out to the sea as do rivers?"

"I suppose Felipe, that they must empty out someplace. Possibly into a lake, or perchance the thirsty sand simply drinks the water before it can find its way to the sea."

"Perhaps, brother," Felipe suggests, "arroyos are nothing more than dry rivers, rivers that have finally run out of water."

"That is sad to think, Felipe."

"Why do you say?"

"A river, Felipe, is a great conducer of life although in itself the river is not alive. It is sad to believe that such a thing could exhaust its own life-blood, after providing life for fish, frogs, water fowl and all the creatures that come to drink of its waters."

"If it is not alive, Manuel, how can it exhaust its own life-blood? It is merely a thing that has ceased to exist without ever having lived."

"Define life, Felipe."

"Life, my brother, is simple awareness."

"Awareness of oneself, or awareness of others?"

"Awareness is life Manuel. If one has awareness, then he truly is alive and he knows that he lives."

"What if something is not aware that it lives, but others are aware that it possesses life? Does the awareness of others imbue it with life?"

"What do you mean Manuel; how can something live and not be aware that it is alive?"

"Those cicadas that you hear chirping, Felipe, are they aware that they live? And that small cactus plant, is it aware that it can die?"

"Manuel, you think too much my brother. You will make yourself crazy—"

Abruptly Manuel stops; then pointing to the bottom of the arroyo wall he asks, "What protrudes from the side of the arroyo? Is it a chest?"

Both hurry to investigate the dark object jutting from the sandy loam. "It is a chest, Felipe, and it appears solid."

The brothers stare at one another. "Perhaps it is a pirate's chest full of treasure, Manuel!"

"It has been buried deep." Manuel stares up, gauging the distance to the top of the arroyo. "At least two meters deep, my brother. Dead men are buried at that depth. Perhaps we should let it be."

"Nonsense, Manuel. It is too sturdy to be a man's coffin. The flooding last year must have un-lodged it from its place of concealment." With his right hand Felipe rubs the side of the chest that juts from the sandy wall. At once, caked sand breaks away in large chunks.

"This wood is extremely hard and nearly black in color. Look, Manuel, it has a sturdy handle for carrying. It *is* a pirate's chest!"

Manuel stares suspiciously at the dark chest and signs himself with the Holy Sign. "We should let it be, Felipe."

"Nonsense, brother. Go fetch one of the horses. Walk him down the side of the arroyo where it is not so steep. We can tie my good lariat to this handle and use the horse to pull it free from the sand. I will remain here and wait my brother, for if we both leave this great treasure may not be here when we return."

"Felipe, I have a bad feeling—"

"Manuel, my brother. We shall return to Spain wealthy men instead of paupers who travel through this savage land in search of adventure and fortune. We will be able to court and wed proper *señoritas* in the great city of Barcelona, and have children to carry on the family name. Have faith, my brother, go for the horse."

Manuel returns with his horse Santo, a solid white, powerful Arabian stallion with flowing mane and tail. Felipe slips the noose of his lariat over the saddle horn and ties a slipknot to the exposed chest handle. Manuel mounts his horse and urges him along as Felipe anxiously helps by pulling on the lariat. The horse whines nervously, and with a jerk of his powerful neck the chest comes free. Felipe falls on his buttock and lets out a victorious yelp. The white stallion snorts and struts nervously about; Manuel remains in the saddle retrieving his brother's lariat.

"What is it?" Manuel asks, "Is it treasure?"

"There are odd symbols etched on the trunk lid my brother, letters that do not form words, come and see."

"My horse will go no closer, Felipe, I fear that if I dismount he will run away." Manuel is an excellent horseman, but try as he may his Arabian stallion whines and walks backwards each time he urges it closer to Felipe and the treasure chest.

"The only word that I can make out, Manuel, is wrong. *Muló*," Felipe yells out. "The others are just letters, *b-e-n-g* and *b-i-b-a-x-t*."

Manuel considers if the letters his brother has sounded off spell anything. Beng. Bibaxt. And muló. Someone's misspelling of the Castilian word for mule—*mula*? Or perhaps the intention of some semi-literate simpleton to describe someone as *stubborn as a male-mule*, in bastardization of their holy mother tongue!

From his mount Manuel calls, "Can you open the lid, Felipe?"

"It is secured by a great brass lock that has no place to fit a key. Your horse pistol, Manuel, I shall shoot the lock off!"

The ancient wheel-lock pistols were commonly called *horse pistols*. Too big and unwieldy to lug around on your person, as many as four of these heavy pistols were frequently holstered to the horse saddle within easy reach of the rider.

Santo still refuses to go near the chest, so Felipe casually walks up to his brother. Santo snorts loudly and turns completely around, trotting sideways, establishing even more distance from the chest.

"Here is the pistol, Felipe. It is charged and ready to fire. I shall take my horse up the side of the arroyo and tie him there. Wait, my brother, until I return."

Why would anyone secure a chest with a lock that has no place to fit a key? Unless ... Manuel has just cleared the arroyo wall. *Whoever buried the chest did not intend to retrieve it, or to ever remove the contents from within! That is no treasure chest!*

Before he can yell out a warning to his brother, he hears the thunderous boom of his horse pistol deep within the arroyo. Felipe, not yet twenty, is impetuous and cannot wait to share the thrill of his find with his older brother.

Quickly Manuel attempts to wheel his stallion back down. Instantly a loud whinny erupts from deep within Santo's throat and he rears mightily, standing erect on both hind legs. It is simply a tribute to Manuel's horsemanship that Santo does not throw him. Manuel crouches down in the saddle as his horse gallops wildly away. Manuel does not hear his little brother scream.

* * * *

Manuel is worried. Santo has run nonstop for nearly a league. Now he walks him and rubs his neck vigorously to help calm him. It is a wonder that Santo has not injured himself or dropped dead of sheer exhaustion.

"Do not worry my little Santo," Manuel speaks lovingly to his horse. "I will not make you go back down into that arroyo."

Santo vigorously nods his noble head as if in appreciation. The stallion's eyes, wide with apprehension, stare down at his owner.

"I shall walk you back until you have rested enough that I can once again ride you." Manuel promises, "You will not have to go down there again."

What was it that scared Santo? Pistol shots had not frightened him in the past. Had Santo sensed a *culebra*, a snake that Manuel himself had missed? Santo did not like snakes.

By late afternoon Manuel and Santo have returned to the arroyo. Santo again is acting strange, nervous. True to his word Manuel secures Santo some walking distance from the arroyo and he proceeds to walk back calling out, "Felipe. Where are you, my brother?"

This is strange; Felipe's own horse, a fine black Dutch Warm Blood almost seventeen hands high, is nowhere to be seen. Has Felipe ridden off somewhere, perhaps with the treasure chest?

A cold dread gripes Manuel's heart as he nears the arroyo. It is too quiet. Not a sound at all, not even the chirping of the cicadas on this warm summer afternoon.

Cautiously Manuel slides down the arroyo wall and proceeds west. The shadows are already deepening and the air is cooler down below. Manuel does not have far to walk. His brother will either be there with the treasure chest, or not.

Manuel rounds a small bend and sees his brother slumped over the treasure chest. Is he dead?

"Felipe," Manuel cries out in alarm, "My brother! Felipe!"

Felipe stirs!

Manuel runs up to his brother and grips his shoulder. Immediately he pulls his hand away. Felipe's shoulder is strong and muscular; this withered shoulder of skin and bone cannot belong to his little brother!

"¡Hermano," Felipe calls weakly in their native Castilian, his voice hoarse and raspy. "*Gracias a Dios!* You have returned!"

Manuel stares incredulously at the wasted form of his younger brother. His straight black hair is now completely white, his eyes aged and sunken, his face withered. Something stirs within the treasure chest. Manuel stares ominously at the lid. The symbols *are* odd; letters that do not form words.

The shattered lock lies on the ground by his horse pistol; the great ball from his pistol has dented the lid's fastener. Felipe's most prized possession is jammed into the chest's staple securing the hasp and holding the chest lid closed. It is the large sacramental cross of finest silver, which their mother gave Felipe, that secures the lid!

Manuel's face contorts with sorrow and anxiety. "*¿Por qué?*—Why?" He holds the withered body of his brother close asking, "What has happened to you, my brother, what manner of *brujería* did this to you?"

Felipe looks up at his brother and smiling weakly replies, "Not witchcraft, Manuel, I have fought a great battle and I am ... Victorious!"

"Battle my brother?" Manuel quickly looks around. "I see no fallen combatants ..."

Felipe becomes very still and as the last glimmer of light fades from his aged brown eyes he proclaims, "*La Muerte*, Manuel, I have ... defeated her! I am victorious. I have wrestled *Death* back into her chest!" Those were Felipe's final words.

* * * *

When Nieves finished reading the journal the smoke from *cigarillos* and cigars was thick in the cantina. The men stared vacantly at one another. One by one they seemed to come awake as if they had been dreaming of the great adventure in the newfound land of New Spain, the very place they now called ... *home*.

RANGERVILLE NIGHT

by Janet R. Wilder

Palms bow to the wind
Grackles grasp their perches tight
A full moon sails in a clear dark sky
… then comes the change in the light.

Fog grows and glows like a living thing
Swirling, blowing, densely white
Fog that deadens nocturnal sounds
… then hoofbeats shatter the night.

Horses racing hard and fast
Hooves pounding, left and right
Hell-bent horsemen from the fog emerge
… riding onward towards the fight.

Men riding upright, tall and lean
Coats stream out behind in flight
Men who were long ago buried and mourned
… Texas Rangers show their might.

MURDER AT THE SANTA MARGARITA CROSSROADS

by Mona D. Sizer

Back in the old, lawless days of the Rio Grande Valley, only a couple of decades after Willacy County was created, a commissary for Gulf Coast Irrigation Company workers was built at the crossroads designated on the maps as Santa Margarita. My mother always called it Meade's store, and sometimes we would drive there for bread or sugar. It was only four miles from our farm.

My mother and grandmother sat in the front seat of the Chevy while I stood on the hump of the driveshaft tunnel with my arms on the back of the seat. All the windows would be open, and my hair would be blowing in the cool evening air. Always we went there after dark, or so I recollect. But my memory may be faulty since I was only five.

The owner was W. H. Meade, who looked like the picture book image of Buffalo Bill Cody. Whether he was a real cowboy from the Wild West, I never knew. He looked like one with his white moustache and neat white goatee. His long white hair flowed over his shoulders. I'd never before seen a man with long hair.

At one time he had served as judge in Raymondville, the seat of Willacy County. Now his civic duties were behind him, for he was a storekeeper. Over his white collarless shirt, he wore black suspenders. They were also very interesting because I'd never seen any before. Every man I knew wore a belt to hold his pants up. Beside his brass cash register, Meade had a big glass apothecary jar filled with horehound candy drops. He would always hand me one with a big smile as he rang up our purchases.

"What do you say?" my grandmother would ask.

"Thank you, Mr. Meade." Then, my manners minded, I'd pop it into my mouth.

I didn't particularly like horehound drops. Horehound was a kind of mint that people boiled to make cough drops. They tasted like medicine. But they were somewhat sweet, like candy, so I dutifully sucked on it.

More interesting were the numbers that popped up behind the glass window in the top of the cash register. Our purchases were never more than a few cents. Bread was a nickel. Kraft pimiento cheese, a dime. He stocked apples in a two-sectioned box and soda crackers in a big tin. We could also purchase dried beans from a barrel, sugar from a huge sack, corn meal, and flour. The farmers from San Perlita sold him a little of their extra produce regularly including some butter and milk, but we never bought that. We had cows of our own.

His store really didn't have much for sale. In the middle of the floor were some sturdy oak tables with shirts and overalls and a few Panama straw hats. He generally stood by his cash register behind his single counter while the customers select the proper size. A few canned goods were lined up on the shelves behind him as well as a supply of flashlight batteries and lamp wicks. He also sold gallon cans of kerosene for lamps.

A big Lady Grace pickle jar sat on the opposite end of the counter from the cash register. I remember those huge pale yellow-green pickles. They were so sour that one bite would pinch my mouth tight.

Years later, someone told me that he also made whiskey that he kept in jugs behind the counter. He probably sold it to preferred customers only.

About a year after the store opened, we arrived one night to be introduced to a young woman named Teresa. She was really young. Younger than my mother. And very dark-complexioned with long black hair hanging down to her waist in back. I'd never seen hair like that, and I studied it almost as carefully as I'd studied Mr. Meade's white hair and moustache and goatee.

I wondered if she was his daughter though they didn't look a bit alike. Then I decided that she must be his wife. I think I even called her Mrs. Meade, and she didn't correct me. Mother and Mammaw usually chatted with her while Mr. Meade filled the orders. Mr. Meade seemed very fond of her. Once he put his arm around her as he escorted us to the door, and they waited until we drove away in the dark. I didn't find that unusual. I knew that she was a Mexican woman who spoke very good English. She was very pretty and had very pretty hair. I was quite envious.

Once on the way home, my mother and grandmother had discussed Mrs. Meade. The rumor was that she had another husband in Kenedy County to the north. I was sure that couldn't be true. After all, she was married to Mr. Meade, and she was always with him in his store. I didn't know much, but I knew that a woman couldn't have more than one husband, and a man couldn't have more than one wife.

Meade was a true Valley pioneer who boasted a long history of defending himself and his property against intruders. It was well-known that he kept several pistols hidden about the store.

His neighbors and customers gossiped about the time he'd actually sold a sack of dried pinto beans with a loaded revolver amongst them. Somehow he had measured up the beans with his big scoop without noticing he'd slid a small gun into the sack.

The person who got the weapon returned it for more beans. He and Meade laughed together. Everyone laughed about it. And the story spread. Pretty soon most of the people in the Valley knew that thieves had better beware. Meade was armed.

But his guns didn't prevent the tragedy. One night a crime was committed that was never solved.

The people of Willacy County were told a plausible story of Mexican bandits who had crossed the border. The story even went that they galloped up on horseback to steal and murder. The old man and his young beautiful wife alone at the crossroads were easy prey.

Whether the bandits came on horseback or in a pickup truck, they broke into Meade's store on Saturday night during cotton-picking season, a time of the year when they could be assured that he had taken in plenty of money. It was also a time when a few more strangers wouldn't have been noticed among the migrants. They cleaned out the cash register. And then, so the story goes, they demanded more and began searching. Almost immediately they found his stash of whiskey and began to pass his jugs around.

Drunk and mean, they threatened him.

Meade said he didn't have any more money.

They didn't believe him. They said they knew he had money hidden. They hit him across the face and beat him down with one of their pistols.

Then one of them started to strangle Mrs. Meade. She screamed and fought.

When his wife was attacked, the old man struggled to his feet and went for one of the several pistols hidden in the barrels in his store. The bandits were ready for him and shot him with his own gun. Then they took their loot and escaped, kidnapping Mrs. Meade and taking her into Mexico never to be heard of again.

And that is one story—the story for children. But why would a gang of Mexican bandits ride fifty miles north from the river to rob a lonely store? Why not rob the grocery store in Raymondville itself where there was much more money not well protected?

But perhaps there is another story. Perhaps the bandits only took the money to disguise a more sinister purpose. Now that I am no longer a child, I have heard a scandal.

Mrs. Meade was not Mrs. Meade at all. She was the wife of another man, a Mexican rancher, who lived in a big house in northwestern Kenedy County. He was a ruthless man who had treated his young wife badly. She had left him and fled to Meade because he said he would take care of her. And so he had done.

If they had been unhappy, the rancher might have forgotten all about her, but they were happy. Their happiness flew in the face of his manhood, his *machismo*, so he came to get her back. If he had to kill the man who had taken her, he would. Perhaps he had planned to do so all along. How simple to order some of his armed range riders into a couple of pickups and come for his revenge. And Meade died under his guns.

The truth will never be known.

Where did the story of what happened there that night come from?

Like the rumors of the Meade's pistol in the bean barrel, it circulated. From person to person, whispered into eager ears, accompanied by scandalized "oh's" and "ah's." Many people heard confused stories of robbery, assault, vengeance, and murder. And both have been passed down for more than half a century.

What is significant is that almost no investigation was made to solve the crime. Local law came to survey the scene, but they soon left without looking for a single footprint or searching out a single clue. A Texas Ranger with a shiny badge was seen in town as well. He called on the sheriff. They spent some time in the café over chili and beer. Then he departed without so much as a ride out to Santa Margarita. No border manhunt was staged. No tracks were followed into the brush. No murdering kidnappers were ever caught and brought to trial.

The delta of the Rio Grande was a wild land in 1940. Mexican ranchers had no recourse to the law enforced by Texican county judges. Personal feuds were more often than not settled by the parties involved. The attitude of most men was that a Willacy County sheriff should look the other way rather than get involved if a man stole another man's wife. If the offended man could get his wife back, then more power to him. If the offender got in the way, he had to take what came.

Men considered that rough justice had been done. No one was complaining. Perhaps not even Mrs. Meade who might have gone back to being a *señora* with a little secret smile of pride that she had been worth fighting for. Perhaps she believed that the better man had won.

No one will ever know. The bad old days of the Valley hold their secrets forever.

VIPER'S REVENGE

by Verne Wheelwright

Some stories of mysterious death seem so logical, so plausible, and they are often told about someone the teller of the story actually almost knew. This story is one I was told many times by the "old-timers" as I grew up in a very small town in Idaho, where everyone really did know nearly everyone else in town.

I heard this story again when I lived in Oregon, and then once more here in the valley of the Rio Grande.

David had been working all morning repairing fencing around the pasture just west of his two-story family home. The weather was warm for early spring, but a strong wind had been blowing most of the day. He came back to the house at lunchtime and ate the meal his wife, Maria, had prepared for him with the obvious enthusiasm of a hungry man. While they ate, he mentioned to her that he had killed a medium size rattlesnake that morning, probably about four feet long, the first one David had seen that spring. "Whapped 'im with a fencepost."

This was quite a change from their first years on the farm, when they encountered large rattlers nearly every week. David felt that the family's active working of the farm had probably sent the large snakes looking for quieter surroundings.

People on farms had differing opinions about snakes, and particularly rattlers. They knew that snakes ate rodents and other costly pests, but a rattler was a risk to children and livestock, as well as to adults that failed to give them wide berth. It was said that in the heat of late summer, when they were shedding their skins, rattlers couldn't see, so they struck at anything that came close. Men often carried pistols loaded with shot, which would spread quickly and hit a small target without careful aim. Women working in their gardens were adept with their sharp edged hoes, and would separate most any snake that came within reach into two wiggling parts. Most felt that the best snake was a dead one.

After lunch, David pulled up the straps of his overhauls, put his broad-brimmed straw hat on his head, held Maria in a warm hug and kissed her before he strode off to the barn where he had more repairs to do. On the way, he stopped at the tool shed to pick up a pry bar, an adjustable wrench and large bolt, then went on to the barn.

In those times, most farmers had a few cows, enough to provide milk, cream and butter for the family, and often a few gallons to sell to the local "creamery." The creamery would send a truck out at regular times to pick up the large, five gallon milk cans that the farmers placed at the side of the road in the morning, and leave some empty cans for the farmer to refill. When the cows came into the barn for milking each morning and evening, they would go to a large wooden trough where the farmer would strew hay for them to eat. They would put their heads through an opening between two upright posts, often 2x4s, in order to get to the hay. One of these uprights would pivot from the bottom, allowing the farmer to close the gap between the two uprights just enough that the cow could not remove her head while he was milking. She could move her head up and down to eat, she just couldn't back up. For someone sitting on a stool beside the cow, milking into a bucket that was under her, this was important. The whole point of this is that the device for keeping the cow in place is called a stanchion, a word that is not familiar to most folks these days.

As he worked to replace the pivot bolt on the old stanchion, David braced himself with one foot against the nearby wall, pushing hard to line up the large bolt through the hole in the two-by-four. Once the bolt was in place, he threaded on the nut and tightened it. When his repair of the stanchion was complete, David stood, picked up his tools and walked slowly toward the big door at the end of the barn. The fresh air would feel good.

Later that afternoon, Maria made iced tea, filled a fruit jar, and took the slightly bitter brown liquid to David in the barn. But he was nowhere in sight. She expected to find him from the sound of his work, but the barn was silent, except for the sound of wind moving through the old structure. She thought he would be working at the milking stanchions, but he wasn't there, so she called his name, but there was no response. As she walked on through the barn, looking up into the lofts and peering at the far recesses, she called his name again, but again, no answer.

Thinking he might be at the big door where the cows entered the barn every evening, she went there, slid the door open and froze! David was lying on the ground, apparently unconscious. Frantic, she knelt beside him, urgently calling his name. He tried to answer, but although his lips moved as though he was trying to speak, no sound could be heard. His eyes remained closed. She knew she couldn't move him to the house herself, so she told him she was going to phone for help.

This all took place many years ago, when phone calls took longer to make because all calls went first to a central operator who then put your call through. The advantage of this system was that the operator, often known simply as "Central" usually knew where to find the local doctor. Doctors went to the homes of patients who were too sick or too contagious to come to the doctor's office. In emergencies, "Central" would call the home of the last patient where she knew the doctor had been, then call the next stop or the next until she found him. Ambulances were common only in the cities, and getting a doctor out to a farm home took time. Although David and Maria's neighbors were alerted by "Central," by the time help arrived, it was too late for David.

What had happened to take David's life so suddenly? David was a healthy man, or had been. There was no sign of injury, no bleeding, not even a bruise. When the doctor arrived, a closer examination revealed that David's right leg was swollen, and when his boot was cut off, the foot was discolored. Almost as though he had bitten by a rattlesnake, but there were no signs of a bite, or even an injury.

When Maria was told, she remembered that David had reported his encounter with a rattler that morning. But he hadn't been bitten! He had killed the poisonous viper with a fence post. The doctor was puzzled, then asked Maria to show him where David had been working that morning. It didn't take long to find the dead rattler, its head crushed into the imprint of David's boot. Mystified, the doctor walked back across the pasture to the farmhouse. Later, he examined David's boot, which had been cut completely open along the inside seam in order to remove it from David's swollen foot.

The doctor looked at the boot carefully, peering inside, and examining the sole. He asked for a sharp knife, then carefully cut along the line where the boot joined the sole, laying the inside of the boot open. There, just protruding through the sole could be seen the tips of a pair of fangs.

As I said at the beginning, this is a story I heard many times, and in different versions. In one variation, a young ranch hand, proudly wearing a brand new pair of boots, encounters and kills a large rattler. (The rattlesnakes in these stories were always very large). As the still-wriggling snake lay dying, the young hand finished him off by stomping the snake's head into the flat rock outcropping where it had been lying in wait for a meal. That night, while the young hand slept in the bunkhouse, someone stole the new boots of which he was so proud.

Several days later another ranch hand was found dead where he had been working to mend fences. He was wearing the stolen boots, and the rattlesnake's fangs had worked through the sole of the boot and killed him.

This version offers a sense of tough Western justice to the tale. There are other variations on this story, in some cases more than one person dies from the same pair of boots, but all versions have in common the dead rattlesnake and the fatal boots, and all arrive at similar conclusions. The variety of stories based on this single plot is limited only by the imagination of the storyteller.

THE DEVIL'S GOLD

by Sandra Vela

The love of money is the root of all evil. Don Carlos believed in that terrible power until the day he died. That day made a believer out of his son Juan. Money, especially in the form of gold coins, had a force of its own.

The family of Don Carlos lived a hard life, not unlike others in their same social class, on the arid brush land known as El Valle. The dust blown ranches were scattered apart almost by repulsion. Only the prickly and tough survived. Don Carlos was one of those.

His family had lived on Rancho La Canica more years than he could remember. The ranch hardly resembled a shiny marble, which was what its name meant. One could scarcely call what they did on the land farming. It was more like beating the ground, tossing in a handful of seeds, and watering it with nothing more than sweat and spit. Nothing had grown on the farmland for years.

The people who remained had held their own during the Mexican Revolution rather than fleeing to the north as many had done. Few had come back to reclaim their land, so Don Carlos, like others, soon moved into the sturdier abandoned homes. Many did not return to their homes because they believed the stories that the ranch was haunted or cursed. They warned Don Carlos. They'd seen the flames rise in the dark of night.

"There's something buried there that belongs to the devil."

But Don Carlos was young and in love. The structure he and his new bride Elena moved into was more like a well-built *jacal* or hut. When Don Carlos laid claim to their new residence, he found a shiny coin on the dirt floor. The young man and his bride believed the coin was a sign of good fortune for them, but they were wrong.

Close to the end of his life, Don Carlos succumbed to the fear of leaving the place he'd always referred to as "el infierno" without the benefit of a sprinkling of holy water. His faith remained buried along with his young wife and three children he'd laid to rest over twenty years before. He dreamed of her often, but that night he'd seen her standing at the foot of his bed looking at him with her warm smile. His heart leapt, as the striking vision rekindled his memory of his querida.

"Elena," he gasped, "have you come for me?"

Don Carlos hadn't spoken her name since her death. That night he was not frightened by the apparition but felt her love and concern for him. Her face shone with a luminescent glow, which seemed perfectly familiar to him. He used to stand where she stood now and look at her surrounded by the very same glow of moonlight as she slept soundly. On those nights, he had no trouble believing in God.

The ghost of Elena smiled at him; then held out the shiny pendant she'd worn around her neck since the day they moved into the house.

"The coin."

He remembered how he'd put it in her hand as she lay cold in her coffin. "You still have it, *mi amor*," his voice a tender whisper. "It was supposed to be our fortune, but with you gone, there was no reason to keep it here."

Just as in life, Elena said so much with her deep, dark eyes. She seemed sad to Carlos. He couldn't bear the thought that she might be sad to see what had become of him. Her gaze mesmerized him and the deep love he had for her welled up in his throat.

"Don't worry, *Querida*. I'll be joining you soon, but I am now so old and dry, no longer fit for one as beautiful as you." Don Carlos wanted only to be near Elena again. The sight of her brought him comfort, but he feared he had not lived a life good enough to deserve eternity with her.

"*Mi Carlitos*," she whispered. "You know what you need to do." She nodded her head and held out the pendant he had given her so long ago. Then she turned and walked through the back wall of their hut and disappeared.

"Don't go, *mi amor*," he wailed. He saw the moonlight streaming through the roof against the wall where she had vanished. He cried out to her. "Don't leave me. I've waited so long to be with you again." He pounded his bony fist against the mud-packed wall and sobbed just as he had on the day that she died. It was an ache too deep to heal. This place had truly been a curse. He slumped down to the floor and found the gold coin hanging from the chain.

The next morning, he sent his son, Juan, to the church in Ciudad Guerrero to make an offering with hopes of attracting a priest to give him his last rites. He knew the coin was his ticket back to Elena. Now, more than anything else, even if he had to face the devil himself, he was willing to do whatever the church asked of him, no matter what.

"Swear to me that you'll go to the church to make the offering," Don Carlos pleaded with his son.

Juan hesitated uncertain of his father's sudden urgency. "But, Papa—"

The old man grabbed Juan's arm pulling him down with unexplainable strength until he was staring deep into the eyes of his son. "The coin," Don Carlos wheezed. "Take the coin."

"What coin?"

Don Carlos grabbed Juan's wrist and pressed the coin into his hand.

"What is this, Papa? Where did you get something like this?" He turned the lustrous coin in his hand. Juan had never seen anything like it in his life. "It's real gold," he said bewildered.

Don Carlos' grey-blue eyes fixed steadily on Juan's soft brown ones. He had never told anyone, not even Juan, about the coin. Don Carlos had not spoken much to Juan over the years about his mother, and Juan, out of respect for his father, had never questioned his reasons.

"Your mother brought it to me last night," he finally said, "but it does not belong to us."

Juan nodded, his thoughts still tangled and confused. He waited in stunned silence, hoping Don Carlos would provide more of an explanation for the urgency of his request, but he only gave instructions.

"You must go to the church and give the coin as an offering to the priest," Don Carlos ordered. "And make confession, *hijo*. You need to do that first."

He coughed and slumped back down in the cot. "It must be done," he gasped. "Promise me."

"Sí, Papa. Calm yourself. I will make the offering. I'll go," he shushed the frail man who released his grip and dropped back into the bed exhausted and relieved.

Not for a long time had the priests traveled the path between the big church in Brownsville and the remote ranchos in Roma. Many of the neighboring ranchos, especially La Canica, had not done much spiritually or financially through the years to attract the horseback riding Oblates to venture too far off the well-worn trail. The land and the people were all but forgotten.

Juan, like others from the ranchos, had seen the flames rising from the rocks in the surrounding desert. Some believed the land was cursed. Juan did not believe the stories he had heard a thousand times, old stories based on nothing but superstitions passed down through the generations.

The stories told of pacts made with the devil for gold. If one saw flames rise around places where no fire actually existed, gold was buried there.

Those that had been tempted to dig it up brought its curse into their homes. They suffered for their greed, as did the land. This curse, would not end until the gold was once again buried where the devil had left it.

These stories warned others to stay away from seeking out the treasures. To be faithful and poor was the only way to survive. The penitents made their prayer pilgrimages to La Lomita Mission, which had been the Oblate's half-way stopping point in the old days to pray for faith and mercy.

Juan shook his head confounded. How had it come to this? His father had never been a religious man. In fact, he had been vehemently opposed to the practice of religion for as long as Juan could remember. Juan recalled that few things could summon the demons out of his father more than the Catholic religion.

Juan also had no memory of his mother. She had died soon after he was born.

With her had died his father's spirit. Women who cared for him said Don Carlos had lost his faith. To lose faith was to lose all hope. It was a mystery to them how long he had survived with that torment.

The women had been kind to Juan providing what they could in the way of religious education; as much as Don Carlos would allow. Juan had learned most of what he believed about the world of spirit from nature. He had spent countless hours in the remote wilderness.

The land surrounding the ranch was full of life and abundance if one just took the time to notice. Unlike most young men his age, Juan had no desire to leave the ranch. He felt close to his ancestors in this place. He spent time among the graves of his family, the old ones that never knew him, his infant brothers, and the mother he'd never known. He felt closer to them, than even to his father who lived and breathed among the living, a shell of a man left vacant by too much loss.

Ciudad Guerrero was a city in much decline since its colonial heyday, but a city, nevertheless, with a church. The region, once an important player in the booming colonial center of commerce, boasted Spanish imperial influence. Cuidad Guerrero had once been earmarked for land grants and settlements, touted as a bastion of Spanish rule. The streets of this frontier expansion were built with gold and silver minted nearby in the late1700's. Not much was left of those riches, however, only the legends and myths around the fortunes both gained and lost in three short generations.

"Have you seen Father Prado?" asked Sister Carla scurrying through the sanctuary of the Mission of Saint Ignacius Loyola, the patron saint of Guerrero.

"No, sister," answered the janitor. "Maybe he fell asleep." He smirked as he pointed with his broom to the confessional booth at the opposite end of the church. "It's been kind of quiet today."

Sister Carla half believed him, and she didn't like the reputation Father Prado was getting around the church for being lazy. She squinted suspiciously. Was he there? She didn't want to disturb Father Prado if he was at prayer, but he had been missing for a while, and she had other things to do besides keep track of lazy, young priests, especially those that came from wealthy families and had little interest in the needs of the poor.

Just then, the sanctuary doors opened letting in the blinding noonday sun. Sister Carla and the janitor looked up at the glare, and in walked a hunched figure of a man. Once he closed the door behind him, he removed his hat, dipped his hands into the holy water, and made the sign of the cross. They saw the man step into the confessional and close the fabric screen behind him.

"He's doing God's work," she reprimanded the janitor curtly, "and you should be doing yours!"

The janitor shrugged and continued pushing his mop across the marble floor. It wasn't the first time he'd been scolded by a nun, and it probably wouldn't be the last.

Juan cleared his throat as he knelt against the hard wooden platform in the confessional. He could hear the priest on the other side of the panel, snoring softly. Juan's eyes had not quite adjusted to the darkness of the booth, and he rubbed the cool drops of holy water across his face careful not to wipe them off completely as he made the sign of the cross several times across his face and chest.

"Bless me father, for I have sinned." He paused expecting the usual response, but heard nothing. Juan shuffled his knees and cleared his throat hoping to rouse the snoring priest from his nap without causing him any embarrassment. As he shifted his knees, he felt a strange heat in his pocket where he'd placed the coin.

"Bless me, father, for I have sinned," he repeated in a voice much louder than Juan felt comfortable using in a church.

Still no response.

Juan wasn't sure what he should do. *Maybe I should just start*, he thought. His eyes could now see a figure begin to stir against the wall of the confessional. *Good*, he thought, *maybe now we can get to business.* "Bless me, father, for I—"

The priest sat up startled and blurted, "Yes, yes—I mean—how long has it been since your last confession?"

Juan cleared his throat. "It's been many years, father. I really don't remember how long. My dying father sent me to make this offering," he explained as he slipped the coin, now more than warm from the heat of his body and glowing faintly, through the half moon slot in the partition. He heard the priest gasp.

On the other side of the partition, the startled priest tried his best to remain calm. He'd heard about the treasures buried in the area, but this was the first time he'd actually seen one of the coins. This was what he had been hoping to find. These were the very coins his father had told him about that had financed the colonization of this region, Spanish gold, *escudo* coins valued at sixteen times that of silver *reales*! He knew his history, and he knew if there was one, there had to be more!

"Where did you get this coin?" asked Father Prado. The coin was perfectly preserved, except for a small hole at the top, a marking he planned to look up in his books. He gripped the coin in his fist and was comforted by its warmth. For this very reason he'd taken on this God forsaken post in *la frontera* in the first place. He knew a treasure was hidden here. Now it had found him!

"It belonged to my father," Juan explained. "He wanted me to bring it here to the church."

"We must go to him then!" Father Prado exclaimed. Juan was startled by the man's insistence that they leave immediately to visit Don Carlos.

* * * *

Father Prado and Juan arrived late in the evening to the ranch. They found Don Carlos barely breathing on his cot.

"Papa," Juan whispered reverently to his father. "Here is the priest," he motioned to Father Prado to come closer.

"Leave me alone with your father to take confession," Father Prado instructed. His eyes adjusted to the dark, dusty room as he knelt at the old man's side.

"I knew you'd come," whispered Don Carlos. "I knew you'd come once you saw the coin."

"Where did you get such a coin?" He asked in his most unctuous voice.

Don Carlos managed a toothless grin. "I see you recognize your treasure?"

Father Prado blinked his surprise. *Was this old man delirious? How could he know the real reason for the priest's visit?*

Don Carlos took a deep rattling breath and when he exhaled, Father Prado saw a plume of cold vapor escape from Don Carlos' mouth. It chilled the room, and the coin in the priest's pocket grew hotter.

This was no ordinary peasant farmer wanting absolution from the church. Father Prado knew he was not there to grant it, anyway. He felt his temper grow hotter as the coin singed his leg.

"Do you have something to confess," he whispered piously hoping to coax a confession from Don Carlos. "You don't want to die with sin on your soul, Don Carlos." Prado reached for the old man's neck impatient for an answer. He wasn't going to let Don Carlos die before he knew where the rest of the treasure in gold *escudos* was stashed. "Tell me where you've hidden the rest of it!" he demanded.

Don Carlos cowered in the bed as the priest's shadow loomed over him. "That was the only one, padre, I swear."

He's stupid enough to die without telling a soul like so many of the old ones who believed the legends. What idiots! Didn't they realize what these coins were worth? "Where have you hidden it?" he growled as one possessed. "There have to be more!"

Prado watched as the old man's face began to glow with an eerie light. He heard what sounded like a heavy stone fall against the roof of the hut and rumble down the back wall. Father Prado looked up startled. He stared up at the roof beams and tried to follow the vibrations that shook down dust and debris all around him.

The room began to glow with a bluish light. Father Prado felt the air sucked out of his lungs as a tremendous force pushed against his chest, lifted him off the ground, and propelled him against the back wall with a deadly thud. The mud plastered walls crumbled from the impact.

The priest hung like a prize suspended against the wall. A post from the rough-hewn wall jutted clean through his back and protruded from his chest.

The commotion rushed Juan into the room. His eyes took a moment to adjust. *What had happened?* He saw Father Prado's body bowed backward impaled on the timbers. His eyes and mouth gaped in an expression of horror, an expression that Juan would never forget.

As Juan brought the priest down from the splintered post, Father Prado released his last guttural breath and earthly words. Juan heard him exhale, "The gold!"

Juan turned and caught the glint of hundreds of gold coins, which tumbled from the crumbling wall and lay strewn across the dirt floor at their feet.

* * * *

Juan buried the priest along with his secret and the gold, in the brush land surrounding the rancho. No one from La Canica thought to question Juan about the events of that night. No one would believe that Don Carlos had summoned a priest even on his deathbed. No one had seen Father Prado leave with Juan from the church that day. No one had seen them arrive at the rancho late that night.

No one even questioned why Juan's hair seemed to turn white overnight. The people of the rancho had seen such things happen before when one of their people had suffered a deep grief or a big fright. To them, death was an un-welcomed visitor no matter when it called. They reached for their rosary beads in times like these to pray for the soul of the dearly departed. For Don Carlos, they knew they needed to pray extra hard.

Juan buried Don Carlos next to their beloved Elena. She was the only one Don Carlos had ever really loved. Juan hoped to find that kind of love with another some day.

On cool foggy mornings, Juan could see his parents walking arm in arm, among their gravestones whispering to each other like carefree lovers unencumbered by the trappings of earthly existence. They were at peace, and Juan liked coming to visit their graves.

On those dark desolate nights when Juan saw flames rise and glow in the distance, he knew to stay away from the beacon. He told the story of the devil's gold warning others of its sinister force until he, too, was a very old man.

QUINTA MAZATLAN

by Marjorie Johnson

The wind whistled through the thick adobe walls of the abandoned home, which had been damaged but not destroyed by Hurricane Beulah in September 1967. There were leaks in the roof and evidence of vandalism, but the sturdy, rambling hacienda was still impressive. In the late 1960s, many people wandered through the tangled brush that surrounded the home and examined the buildings built around a large swimming pool. Through a window one could see a rope ladder dangling from the ceiling, leading to a second floor room. The place was said to be haunted, that the ghost of old Jason Matthews roamed through the house.

Matthews was an adventurer, world traveler, and veteran of World War I with service in 11 foreign countries. A soldier of fortune, he had fought with Lawrence of Arabia and had been an aviator, explorer, writer and photographer. He was also a music composer and was a member of the American Society of Composers, Authors and Publishers (ASCAP).

Originally from Charlottesville, Virginia, Jason Matthews had an affinity for the Southwest. Then living in Mexico, he was looking for a place to build a permanent home. He decided that the home site had to be at the crossroads of the Western Hemisphere, from which he could oversee his far-flung interests.

A map and air lanes told Matthews that this spot lay in the Rio Grande Valley of Texas. The land he found for his home was just a street away from what is now the McAllen-Miller International Airport. At the time, the four and one-half acre site south of the city was covered in Tamaulipas thornbrush, far from prying eyes.

Marcia Matthews, educated and talented in her own right, was from Warren, Pennsylvania, where her family was in the wholesale hardware business, with holdings in the Pennsylvania oilfields. The Matthews' extensive travels and support for their other activities was largely from this wealth. Though Marcia had a son and daughter from an earlier marriage, the Matthews did not have children of their own.

The Matthews moved to McAllen in the mid-1930s and set about to build their home of adobe. Jason wanted to prove to Texans that adobe is an economical, durable and handsome material for home building. After lengthy experiments, Jason developed a formula that was so durable and water-resistant that he built his swimming pool with them as well. He never revealed his secret adobe formula.

The swimming pool was built first. The studio that became Matthews' retreat for more than two decades came next, and then the handsome residence itself. All were built from the adobe bricks that were made and dried on the site, plus generous use of Talavera tile from Puebla, Mexico.

They named their home "Quinta Mazatlan," which means "place where deer abound." The house was set among elegant tall palms that reach above the rambling adobe structure. The cupola on the front of the house was decorated with the Azul tiles that also appear throughout the building. The windows brought the sunlight inside to a reading room that included well-worn classics from their extensive library, plus current newspapers and magazines from over the United States and beyond.

Many years later, a friend from those years, Lillian Leonard, recalled that they worked very hard on the house. Mrs. Leonard was 91 in the mid-1980s when she was asked to share memories of her friendship with the Matthews.

"They built the house well. It had good design and the furniture was lovely. They were both such good, genuine people, but they were different. He'd walk to town in his English walking shorts and a stick. They always had lots of company—people out to swim or just look at the house."

"He didn't work, nothing I know of. I don't think he ever worked at a job down here. But he worked hard at writing and reading books. And he'd go into meditation. A trance. Just looking off into space. You'd come in the room and he'd not even know you were there. Then in a little while he'd snap out of it."

"He had a room over the top of the long building in back. It had a knotted rope he climbed up. Then he pulled the rope up back of him so nobody could bother him. He did lots of writing and publishing. And he worked in the greenhouse—some kind of research on growing tomatoes in water. I never understood it all, but I know he spent a lot of time on it."

Among his writings was a book of poetry, *Flame and Melody*. In the Author's Foreword, Jason wrote:

> It is not intended that Flame and Melody should be read by either the very old or the very young. The very old, because the years have brought them the quiet peace of a heart that beats as a bass drum, keeping time, but no longer marching in the parade. Better they never turn the pages of this book than find some passage that rips open the wounds of half-forgotten dreams, letting them bleed with memory.
>
> To the very old and the unmarried young, I say, put down this volume. Wrap the shawl of old dreams and young dreams close about you and hurry away. *Flame and Melody* is not intended for your eyes, for it is raw with the heartbeat of your yesterdays and your tomorrows yet to come.

Published in Chicago in 1953, the opening page of the book states that the author's royalty was to be wholly contributed to the Damon Runyon Cancer Fund.

A reviewer of the time, Felix Wittmer, wrote, "The fifty-five poems of *Flame and Melody* are the strong and sturdy testimony of a man of action, a man who does not believe in doing things half way. He has lived a full and rich life, always wholly stirred by extraordinary people and landscapes he encountered, and wholly consumed by love."

In addition to his literary pursuits, Jason was always interested in current events and patriotic activities. The greenhouse research was done in connection with World War II. The Pacific war was hard fought, island by island, with the Japanese making strong gains during the early war years. At the same time, our nation was involved in war in Europe. Supplies and rations were a major problem, and fresh vegetables were practically unknown in many of the fighting areas.

When this need became acute, in his greenhouse at Quinta Mazatlan, Jason Matthews did major research to perfect the art of growing fresh vegetables hydroponically through the use of an enriched liquid base in place of soil.

Extensive studies and research were done during 1942 and 1943. Liquid distribution systems were developed and different liquid formulas were tested to see which gave the most rapid growth. Holding tanks and growing racks had to be developed.

There were many failures, but some plants did well. A breakthrough was made when a new variety of tomato was tested and showed promise. In hydroponic growth culture, this one variety of tomato showed amazing productivity. A tomato plant would produce four to five times as many tomatoes under hydroponic culture as it would in soil culture.

Matthews' work at Quinta Mazatlan was being carefully watched by the U. S. Army. When the tomato growth was proven, the Army took all the research notes, moved rapidly and set up hydroponic growth centers in Guam, which had been recaptured. Based on the research done at Quinta Mazatlan, extensive growing systems were established to provide fresh vegetables and tomatoes to the Pacific troops during the last months of the war.

In the 1940s, the Matthews entertained a great deal, and visitors always enjoyed browsing among the many conversational pieces that they had collected from all over the world. Matthews could tell many an adventure based on each.

"She had the most elegant silver," recalled Mrs. Leonard. "We were out for a dress-up dinner and every piece on the table was sterling silver. Large silver dinner plates. Silver goblets. I'd never seen such a table."

In the 1950s, the couple became seriously and heavily involved in conservative projects and Americanism groups. They were recognized as leaders of conservatism. Together, they organized the Legion for the Survival of Freedom, a conservative organization, and broadcast radio programs dedicated to their pro-American beliefs.

With others, they purchased the old *American Mercury* magazine, which had originated in 1924 under the supervision of H. L. Mencken and was one of the oldest literary digests in America. Marcia handled the editing duties from their McAllen home.

The magazine was distributed by subscription only and, along with the other causes which they supported, drained their finances.

After Marcia's death in 1963, Jason seemed lost without his beloved wife and partner. Alone and deep in debt, he kept the magazine going until his death in December 1964 at age 77. Then the *American Mercury* was moved elsewhere, eventually acquired by a publisher in California.

With Jason Matthews death, an era ended for Quinta Mazatlan. Its elegant days were long gone, and stacks of newspapers and books filled its rooms.

"This house was so beautiful in the beginning, but such a mess at the last," recalled Mrs. Leonard. "In the end they ran out of money. She looked bad, so thin. I just couldn't come out here like I had in the early days."

The property served temporarily as a coffee house, a retreat for youth and young adults, but essentially was left to deteriorate. It stood empty when Hurricane Beulah roared through the area in September 1967.

The storied home was purchased in 1968 by Frank and Marilyn Schultz of McAllen, with a dream of restoring it to its former elegance. Not only did they restore the original craftsmanship, they enlarged the house to nearly 10,000 square feet. They planted exotic flowers, shrubs and trees, while welcoming the re-growth of the native thornbrush.

For almost three decades, Quinta Mazatlan again welcomed local and visiting dignitaries to its spacious home and grounds. "Restoring the adobe home of late McAllen writer Jason Matthews has been a labor of love," said Frank Schultz on the eve the dedication of a Texas Historical Marker on September 1, 1985. "It was in absolute desolate condition when we got there."

Quinta Mazatlan's Schultz era ended in 1998, when he decided to put the estate up for auction. By then it was an oasis in the heart of a growing city, a treasure to be preserved and enjoyed. The City of McAllen won the bid and it has become a home with a mission as the McAllen Wing of the World Birding Center.

The Center officially opened in May 2006 for the public to enjoy. It is right off of 10th Street next to the Four Points Sheraton by the airport. The city expanded the grounds, which now occupy 15 acres of beautifully landscaped birding habitat, a walking trail and a bird feeding station. All buildings have been restored and improved. Its 10,000 square foot hacienda from the 1930s serves as an exhibit and meeting space, with an art gallery and nature exhibits that tell the story of South Texas wildlife. It also has historical exhibits that tell the story of Quinta Mazatlan and the unusual couple who built it.

When the ghost of Jason Matthews wanders through the rooms of Quinta Mazatlan, he is in good company. One of the visitors when Quinta Mazatlan was dedicated as the McAllen World Birding Center site was Father Tom Pincelli of Harlingen, avid birder who writes a popular column for Valley publications.

"What a gift this McAllen WBC is to all of us," he wrote. "Quinta Mazatlan is almost beyond words. The old, renovated hacienda is absolutely stunning and, with its outbuildings, blends harmoniously with the surrounding 15 acres of pre-existing or restored woodlands and meadow."

"Trails meander through the lush vegetation and along the edge of open space, offering the visiting nature aficionado ample access to a variety of habitats. This place, both inside and out, will capture your heart and leave you feeling you have wandered into an enchanted land of more than just good birding."

Jason's ghost also would be pleased at the activities planned for children and families, such as Quinta Mazatlan's Distinguished Speaker Series, "Our Nature Hour." World traveler that he was, including time spent in Mexico, Jason himself would have appreciated the presentation by naturalist Roy J. Rodriguez entitled *Pajaros del Valle/Birds of the Valley*, a talk in a bilingual format for Spanish and English speaking guests about how to bird, where to go and what to wear.

A lifelong resident of the Rio Grande Valley, Rodriguez has enjoyed birding since his youth. He has become one of the most popular and knowledgeable birders in South Texas and leads guided trips in the Valley and Mexico.

And many more interesting speakers and visitors will come, nature lovers all. Indeed, Jason and his ghost would surely be proud of what his beloved adobe hacienda has become, and how many people will enjoy its latest reincarnation.

> You breathe my name
> And there is melody,
> That starts the beating heat
> Of wishing dreams within me.
>
> —(From *Flame and Melody* by Jason Matthews)

FRANK'S TROOPS

by Judy Stevens

Mind you, young man, I never seen them ghosts, so don't you go printin' contrary in your fancy newspaper. Not that I don't wish I could've seen 'em like Frank did. But what's the difference? He's gone ahead of me to Glory. Still the same, between you'n me, I feel left out—like I was blind or somethin' an' thet still annoys me.

Aww, look at me, an ol' lady talkin' nonsense. Shucks, nobody else ever saw 'em, either. But never mind. You're here for the story, ain't ya? Lord above, I could tell it in my sleep—heard it a thousand times from Frank.

My Frank, he loved to tell about the fist time he saw 'em, all lined up longside that little church—you know that one on Military Highway down south a'here? You'll find it easy enough—the ghosts sure'nuff did. Lessee—they call it Our Lady Of Visitation Catholic Church—yes, that's right. Did you know they laid th' cornerstone in a snowstorm? 1880—Yes, I swear! Imagine! No, young man, we're not Catholic. But Frank just loved th' little church, and I loved it 'cause I love Frank. Wish I could see it one more time. You'll take a picture? Oh, that'll be swell!

You know, he was in the war. You know anythin 'bout war? You look so young. Oh, you don't say? Well, I declare! Don't that beat all. You look like a baby t'me. Well, my Frank was over there three long years. Horrible time—worse than the Great Depression. He never spoke 'bout it, but the nightmares—Lord-a-mighty!

He always said th' war gave more'n it took from him. And he came back all in a piece, not like some. Soon's he got discharged, he hightailed it back to marry me. And let me tell you, young man, I waited all that time for him. Yessir. Not like today's sweethearts.

Frank come barrelin' up Military Highway, an' he only made one stop 'long the way, just one. It weren't to no bar, no sir, not my Frank. He went lickety-split to "Our Lady" t' pay respects to the Maker for comin' back all in one piece. He got down on his knees in that purty little place, and he plum lost track of time. By th' time he ran out of thankfulness th' sun was nearly set an' he commenced thinkin' 'bout me an' our future and stood up and was thankful all over again.

An' that's when he saw 'em through the side windows—plain as I see you! There they was, twenty combat soldiers, standin' at attention, lookin' straight at him! He always said the sight took years off his life.

Well, let me tell you, Frank hit the dirt! Then he remembered where he was and decided he'd get his friends back for this joke, even though he had to admit it was a lallapalooza.

He stood up whistling, put his hands in his pockets and looked out the windows.

They was still there, lookin' like they was fresh from battle, but in a clean way. That's when he knew it weren't no joke. Somethin' poked him in the pit o' his stomach like when he first saw a dead man. They was standin' close t' each other now, an' holdin' their helmets all respectful-like, and he could see they was a mix a' some enemy and some ours, an' that they was lookin at him like they was meetin' their sweethearts' fathers for the first time! The more he looked the more he swore they seemed like they was graduated to God's army. Frank always had a grin when he told this part, like it pleased him to see ghosts didn't bear a grudge.

When he first told me this tale, I thought sure that the war had addled his brains, like Mary Jo Louise's cousin. But I was determined to marry him anyway, ghosts and all. At least he didn't see them from drinking, not my Frank. So I ribbed him a little and said they sounded like they needed a leader. Said I'd call 'em "Frank's Troops". Frank liked that. He said they did, too. He never did find out how they got all the way over here, but you know what they say about ghosts, they can walk anywhere. Frank said they musta just followed him home, like lost puppies.

We was married in that church, you understand, so Frank's troops could see us. Don't know why they never ventured beyond that stretch of Military Highway. Frank said he thought it was cause they felt at home there, even after vandals broke in and did damage and the church had t' be boarded up. Frank always says it's important to feel at home if you got no body.

That's all I can tell tonight, young man, and now I'm just plum tuckered out. Frank told the story better, but that's the breaks you get for being young and him passin' to Glory before me. He woulda liked you for sure.

My land! It's practically time for supper—and my pills. So many pills when you get on in years. Why, yes, thank you; of course you can. Anytime. I'll be here. You stay sweet as you are, lad.

Nice young man. Polite too, not uppity like you see on TV these days. He's got me thinkin' though,'bout our troops. D'y' think, darlin', they'll pose nice an' purty for his picture? Ah shucks, I probably said that aloud. They already think I'm addled 'roun here, talkin' ta you like this.

But I won't stop, darlin', 'cause I love your grin.

EL CANTAR DE PANCHO VILLA

by Robin Cate

Clouds smeared the sky.
The sun shone in red.
Wind wouldn't whistle,
Pancho Villa is dead.

Mexico's hero,
Chihuahua's bright star.
Soul of his people
Gunned down in his car.

Who fired the rifles?
The Devil they say—
That's not how it was;
I tell you today.

The men who killed Pancho
on the bride's wedding day
shot him from ambush
at a turn on the way.

They shot the fierce rebel
in body and head
buried him quickly
riddled with lead.

But Pancho was tricky,
not ready to die.
He lifted his death mask,
let out a war cry.

Pancho burst free to haunt
the dark night.
He hunted his killers,
filled them with fright.

His eyes shone like agates.
His mouth smiled revenge.
Pancho rode throughout Mexico
to haunt guilty men.

The killers spent days
in zombie-like trances
lashed by their guilt,
lives without chances.

And, still in the fall
around All Hallow's Eve,
Listen! You're hear them
begging: "Release! Release!"

At midnight look closely.
It's then you will see
Pancho riding the border
upon his black steed.

His voice can be heard—
Sounding in echo,

"Viva Pancho!"
"Viva Pancho!"

"Viva P A N C H O Villa!"

Part II

Crossing Over

THE QUAIL AND THE MESSERSCHMITT

by Hernán Moreno-Hinojosa

As the August heat bore down, the lower Rio Grande Valley of Texas in 2007 was one of the more intimidating parts of the United States. "I don't like being out here, Rene. This place is too damned desolate." Steve looked around him and shook his head.

"This is where the oil is, Steve. That's why we're exploring here."

"Nothing here but cactus, needle grass and rattlesnakes! You see that one back there a little while ago?" Steve shivered. "It had to be a six-footer!"

"More like a seven-footer, Steve." Rene kept both hands firmly on the steering wheel and looked straight ahead. "We'll get to the sand dunes in a bit and you'll see, there's *really* nothing there. Even rattlesnakes stay away. Sand's too gritty, they don't like grit in their food."

"Sand dunes? Out here, in the Valley?"

Rene grinned. "Yup, they call it little Sahara."

"You just made that up," Steve replied shaking his head.

Rene grinned at his friend's chagrin. "Sure, but it does sort of remind you of the Sahara, you know, about thirty-thousand acres of flat lands with low rolling sand dunes. It's all sandy loam."

"And you've been to the Sahara!"

"Yup," he answered, "one year the company sent me out there. Didn't like it. You can't get beer, nor cigarettes and the woman stay covered up. All you can see is their eyes." For emphasis Rene brought his thumb and forefinger up to his face, exposing only his eyes. "Those people have a *thing* for dark-eyed virgins, which is fine I guess, but give me a super model in a bikini *any* old day."

The four-wheel drive Blazer eased over a small rise and descended into a vast expanse of sand. Immediately both men reached for their sunglasses.

Rene grinned as Steve made a low gasping sound. "If I weren't looking at it, I wouldn't believe it. What's happened? The mesquite and cactus is all gone. There's nothing here but sand, far as the eye can see!"

"The boss wants us to check for sinkholes."

"Sinkholes?" Steve asked, a tinge of nervousness in his voice.

"Yeah, sinkholes and quicksand. We're bringing in a triple next week and we want to make sure we don't lose any more equipment to quicksand."

Steve stared nervously at Rene hoping it was just another one of his bad jokes. "There's no quicksand in the dry lands, that's only in the jungle."

"That's wet quicksand. This is dry quicksand. Sand that's so loose it won't support your weight and you sink into it."

"You're shitting me again, aren't you?"

Contemplation washed across Rene's face. "Well," he replied, "I have seen the sand swallow up a Ford F350 double-cab four wheeler."

"Completely?"

"To the cab. Took us all day to dig it out, sand kept rolling back quick as we shoveled it out. Then we had to use a crawler to pull it out of the hole."

Both men stepped out of the Blazer into the relentless sun that superheated the ground. Heat wormed through the soles of their boots burning the flat of their feet. They stood there, on the burning ground, wordlessly surveying the landscape. Heat waves emanated from the sand dunes tinting the entire countryside a shade that can only exist in a locale that is situated just a little too close to … Hell.

Rene expounded, "Sand is funny that way. Sometimes it does swallow things up. I read somewhere that an army of soldiers disappeared in the desert one year. No trace of them has ever been found. *Se los trago la tierra*—it's like the ground just opened up and swallowed them, men, equipment, guns … Everything."

Suddenly Steve pointed. "What is that Rene? There, in the distance?"

Rene adjusted his cowboy hat and squinted to see. Then he removed his sunglasses and holding his right hand over his eyes, stared at the distant object. "Looks like a reflection from something shiny lying in the sand."

"Just an old beer can, maybe?"

"Too far away to be a beer can. It's about a quarter of a mile away so it has to be something bigger. Too small to be a windshield, though." Rene stared at the glare for a moment. "Steve, get the Blazer; let's go check it out."

"You think the sand swallowed up another vehicle?"

"Swallowed something up."

*   *   *   *

KTSA blared the now familiar end-of-World-War-II rhetoric over the shop radio. During his break time Miguel San Roman listened to AM American radio. It helped him perfect his English. Over the mumble of the news coverage Miguel thought he discerned a dim sound. Without thinking he reached with his left hand and turned the radio off.

From a great distance the faint hum of an airplane that approached the small airport just outside of Nuevo Laredo, Tamaulipas in Northern Mexico could be heard. The humming intensified to a throaty roar as the aircraft neared. No small radial engine crop duster, this one, Miguel realized. The staccato pulse of the engine's exhaust exuded power—pure, raw power.

The landing field where Miguel worked servicing crop dusters was located just west of the Texas border and he wondered if an American military plane hadn't crossed the border from their sister city to the east. That happened now and then and with the sky overcast all morning, perhaps a disoriented pilot did cross the border and was even now circling the runway awaiting landing instructions.

Wiping his hands on a red rag Miguel looked up from under the hood of his ancient Ford pickup truck sadly shaking his head. He sighed in exasperation. "I cannot let you die like this, my old friend."

His old truck needed a new radiator so it wouldn't boil over on his way to work. It also needed spark plugs, new wiring and a carburetor kit. They couldn't afford the repairs on his tiny wages with his wife Carmen fat with their first child. Why his cousin across the river earned more money as a busboy in a restaurant than he as head mechanic of this airport! Was there no justice in this world?

Frustrated he stepped outside and looked at the sky trying to see through the cloud cover. Perhaps he could catch a glimpse of the *gringo* fighter plane before the pilot realized he had intruded on Mexican airspace. As soon as the pilot spied the green, white and red Mexican flag flying proudly from their flagpole he would spin his plane around, gun the engine and make a run for the border. After all, the pilot didn't want to create an international incident should someone from the local government complain to the US Air Base commander on the Texas side. A novice pilot didn't need that kind of grief!

Just then the airplane made another pass. The engine's reverberation rattled the tin panels in the hanger where he worked and Miguel tore his eyes from the sky to stare momentarily at the vibrating panels. When he looked back, a gray and black airplane dropped out of the cobalt sky and screeched to a halt on the dirt runway.

With a mighty roar the Messerschmitt *bf*-109-E leap-frogged forward. Instantly Miguel's hands flew up clamping tightly over both ears as the pilot gunned the eighteen hundred horsepower, inverted V-12 Daimler-Benz engine. The plane spun around raising a huge cloud of dust as it came to rest facing the runway ready for a quick getaway.

"*¡Santa Madre de Dios!*" Miguel exclaimed as the dust settled revealing a wraith-like flat gray airplane. "Camouflage," Miguel murmured under his breath, "an armed fighter camouflaged to give the wings the squared off appearance of civilian aircraft."

The wing edges were painted black, but no amount of camouflage could disguise the armament. Miguel stared in awe at the two 20-millimeter automatic cannons suspended from pods beneath each wing. From the nose cone of the Messerschmitt the business end of a third automatic cannon peered menacingly at the sky. And from the cowling of the strange aircraft the barrels of two 7.9-millimeter machineguns, synchronized to fire between the spinning propeller jutted out.

"Those gringos are *loco*," Miguel said to himself making the Sign of the Cross, "to land an armed fighter plane on Mexican soil! The *federales* will consider this an act of hostile aggression—an act of war!"

The heavily grated double-canopy lifted and rolled to the right. Miguel saw a tall lanky man—the pilot—stand and climb out of the cockpit onto the airplane's left wing. A submachine gun was slung beneath the pilot's left shoulder. The pilot looked briefly about before jumping from the wing. As he hit the ground a small white cloud of acrid *caliche* dust erupted around his feet. Casually he raised his right leg, then his left, and he slapped at his pant leggings, shaking the dust off.

Miguel hid behind the left front fender of his pickup truck and reached for the driver's side door. His old .30-30 Winchester was stored behind the seat. Was it even loaded?

"*Amigo*," the pilot called out loudly, strolling lazily toward Miguel.

Miguel hesitated. Carmen needed him alive and well. Even loaded and ready his old .30-30 was no match for the pilot's automatic weapon.

"*Sí*," Miguel replied with a raspy voice, "amigo?"

The pilot grinned as he approached. Miguel noticed that the grin did not reach the pilot's pale blue eyes. This man's entire demeanor greatly disturbed Miguel. It was more than the flat-black submachine gun that dangled carelessly from his shoulder. It was something about the deliberate manner in which he carried himself; something about how his cold blue eyes revealed nothing that filled Miguel with inquietude and a vague feeling of impending doom.

Still grinning the pilot said in heavily accented Spanish, "*Amigo, necesito combustible para mi avion*—Friend, I need fuel for my aeroplane."

With a start Miguel realized that this stranger was not a *gringo*. A gringo would have asked for *gasolina*, not *combustible*. Was he European? Perhaps even ... An *aleman*—a German? What was he doing here? Hadn't the gringos won the big war only three days ago; that's all *la radio* talked about and it was in all the newspapers?

"You speak English?"

Miguel nodded vigorously in affirmation.

The stranger casually reached into the left vest pocket of his gray flight suit saying, "I shall pay you in gold."

Miguel stared suspiciously at the two gold coins, about the size of a US quarter, in the palm of the pilot's right hand. Cyrillic markings were scrawled across the face of the coins. Miguel recognized the odd markings from his university days in Monterrey. He studied there to become a doctor before dropping out to marry Carmen Diaz, the love of his life. Greek or Russian writing, Miguel's heart skipped a beat—this man was definitely not a *Norte Americano*. He did not appear Greek. Russian? Was he a Russian? The gold was real enough and a half an ounce of pure gold could buy many things for Carmen and their baby.

"Pure gold, friend," the pilot persisted, his voice cozening, "a fair exchange for some of your aviation fuel, don't you agree?"

Miguel stared at the airplane quickly calculating that an airplane that size would require perhaps two, or three hundred liters of fuel. A single gold coin that size was more than enough compensation. But two coins were more than generous. Could he trust the pilot? Perhaps he didn't know how much he was paying for the fuel. Or perhaps he was also paying for his silence?

"Take the coins, amigo," the pilot insisted, still grinning, steely-blue eyes focused on Miguel. A mere pittance the pilot realized. Crates of gold fillings liberated from executed Jews and gold coins liberated from the Russians along with art treasure from the museums in Europe were stored in crates in the *Unterseeboot*. How glorious it had all been, plundering from the enemies of the Third Reich! His personal favorite bit of Nazi booty, the Madonna With Child by some famous Fleming painter! Oh, he would have that study in oil even if he had to execute everyone onboard the U-boat to keep it!

The gold felt cold and clammy in Miguel's hand as he slipped the coins into his trouser pocket. He looked over his right shoulder at the fuel truck. "This fuel is too, how do you say it, too ... Too oily," Miguel said. Then looking beyond the pilot at his plane, rapidly explained, "Your airplane has injectors, not carburetors. Perhaps it won't burn this fuel very well."

The pilot stared suspiciously at Miguel. What was the Mexican saying? He spoke too fast. Something about oil, motor oil perhaps? With a final fatal grin the pilot replied, "No amigo, my aeroplane will not require any motor oil."

Miguel nodded once, turned and walked rapidly toward the fuel truck. The sooner he finished, the sooner this stranger would leave with his deadly war machine.

* * * *

Carmen Diaz announced cheerfully, "*Mamá*, I have prepared lunch for Miguel. Fried pork *taquitos* with *pico de gallo*, avocado and cilantro, seasoned just right. I made the flour tortillas fresh like he likes them, and I have a *jarrito* of fresh *frijoles a la charra*." Dancing merrily around the small kitchen she added, "I made enough tacos and beans for everyone, so you don't have to worry about preparing lunch."

Carmen was a slender, attractive twenty-year old with complexion the color of fresh honey. Her luscious black hair was shoulder long and she had big bright brown eyes. Her mother was an older version of Carmen and people who had just met them often mistook them for sisters.

"*Mija*, you are wearing your red dress today."

"Sí mamá," she replied, removing her white apron, "it is Miguel's favorite."

Doña Rosario Diaz smiled at her beautiful daughter. What a blessing to have a daughter like Carmen. She always helped with the cooking and housework even though she was five months along with her pregnancy. And that red dress looked marvelous on Carmen, whose tummy was just beginning to protrude. No wonder Miguel fell hopelessly in love with her. Rosario felt doubly blessed, with Carmen and such a good man for a son-in-law. And now, the baby ... But, what a pity about Miguel's parents!

"I didn't know that Miguel was coming home to eat."

"No mamá; I am going now, to take Miguel his lunch. He left without breakfast and he will be hungry. You know how hard he works, *mamácita*, on those flying machines."

"Míja," Doña Rosario admonished, "wait until your little brother comes home at three. Let him take Miguel his lunch. You are well along with your pregnancy and I worry about you riding in that autobus. The ride is too rough for you, míja, in your delicate condition. Then you must walk that last mile to the airport."

Miguel's parents did not approve of Carmen, even though she was considered the prettiest girl in the *barrio*. They wanted their son to marry a classy, fair-complexioned, tall and sophisticated *dama*.

Carmen is sophisticated, Miguel argued.

She is *mestiza*—of mixed blood, his father countered, and so when they married against his wishes, Miguel San Roman was cut off from the family fortune.

"Mamá, *don* Roberto drives the bus very carefully and if he has only one or two passengers he will detour all the way to the airport so I don't have to walk. He is very kind."

"Yes, he has daughters your age, but míja, please, just wait for little Hector—"

"No mamácita," Carmen interrupted, hurriedly placing the food in a wicker basket, "Miguel didn't have any breakfast. He can't wait until little Hector gets out of school. What kind of wife would I be if I don't see to it that my husband gets his meals on time!"

*   *   *   *

The pilot stared impassively at his wristwatch; it was nearly three o'clock. About now the *quail* would be crossing the international bridge to meet him here, at this landing strip. The pilot surveyed the scene. Bobwhite was right, this landing strip *was* the perfect place to rendezvous. There were no telephone or telegraph wires anywhere. There was that old biplane in the hanger and if the attendant could fly it, he would go for help. The attendant's truck appeared disabled, but there was the fuel truck. *I can destroy the fuel truck from the air with the cowling guns and a short burst from the wing cannons will destroy the hanger with the other truck and biplane.* Picturing the razed airfield the pilot finally smiled. The Mexicans would naturally blame their neighbors to the north for the destruction. Of course, there couldn't be any witnesses. *Stupid Americans! The quail and I shall be long gone before anyone realizes that we were here. Heil Hitler!*

* * * *

Miguel San Roman looked up from the wing tank of the strange airplane. A cloud of dust rapidly approached the landing strip from the main road. He was nearly finished filling the plane with aviation fuel.

Relieved he realized that the vehicle approaching was moving too rapidly to be don Roberto in his old autobus bringing Carmen to see him. Grateful for that he quickly made the Sign of the Cross.

The pilot was still, leaning back on a wooden chair, cradling that deadly submachine gun, watching him fuel the plane. Occasionally he gazed at his wristwatch. Miguel realized that the pilot was impatiently waiting for someone.

"Somebody approaches," Miguel said, gesturing toward the road.

The pilot stood and stared at the approaching cloud of dust. "It is the quail," he answered and looked at his wristwatch. "He is right on time."

* * * *

Carmen called to the bus driver, "Don Roberto, that man in the black car is driving so fast."

Roberto coughed and waved his right hand in front of his face to disperse the acrid caliche dust. The rapidly moving black Ford sedan passed them leaving a blinding cloud of white dust in its wake. "Sí Carmen," he replied, "*se va matando*—he is driving at a breakneck speed; maybe he is going to a funeral, no?"

At his words Carmen made the Holy Sign, wobbling in her seat with the rocking motion of the twenty-four-passenger bus that her friend Roberto drove. The baby kicked and she smiled; her husband's lunch was securely wrapped in the wicker basket on her lap, fresh and warm.

* * * *

The black sedan drove right up to the Messerschmitt, coming to a complete halt behind the tail. A tall, lean man with blue eyes and a full head of white hair rapidly exited. Miguel finished fueling the airplane and jumped from the wing.

The pilot rose from his chair, stood erect, snapped his heels together and saluted the newcomer. *"Heil Hitler!"*

¡A la madre, Miguel realized with a start. *They are Nazis!*

The man from the Ford barely returned the salute. "The hell with that," he exclaimed, "it's all over and done with! Get us to South America!"

"Yes, *Herr Oberst* White!"

While they talked, Miguel furtively mounted the driver's side of the fuel truck and started driving away. As he left the runway, a second cloud of dust appeared. This cloud was moving very slowly.

"Don Roberto!" Miguel realized, his blood ice water in his veins. He looked back. The plane was *still* idling roughly on the runway. Miguel was right. The finely tuned German engine did not like the lower-grade fuel. He had tried to warn the pilot.

"Go away," he urged aloud. "Please, hurry up and leave!"

Miguel drove out of the small airport to intercept the approaching bus. In the outboard rearview mirror of the fuel truck Miguel witnessed the Messerschmitt racing down the runway, then, with a sudden roar, it abruptly became airborne.

The engine continued missing. The pilot struggled to adjust the fuel mixture. Unsteadily the Messerschmitt climbed to a thousand feet, then two thousand feet, three thousand feet and more. The big Damlier-Benz engine backfired loudly. The pilot frantically adjusted the fuel mixture.

"What is wrong with your aeroplane?" Oberst White demanded.

"The fuel, Herr Oberst." With sudden insight the pilot realized what the Mexican had tried to tell him. "It is too ... *too oily!*"

"Wasn't the engine de-tuned to accept a lower octane fuel?"

"Oberst White, I want my aeroplane to be fully combat ready—"

"You idiot! The war is over! Who are you going to fight?"

Finally climbing to five thousand feet of altitude, the Messerschmitt leveled off and began descending in lazy circles.

The ancient autobus and the fuel truck converged just outside of the airport. Miguel leapt from the fuel truck and stared straight up, searching the sky. It was up there hidden among the clouds, perhaps a mile high. The distant drone of the big engine reminded Miguel of the faint buzzing of a horsefly. How he hated those things. *They are like dogs with wings, and they bite like dogs.* It occurred to Miguel that, *the plane's bite is even worse! Those big guns can turn human flesh into mincemeat!*

He rushed inside the bus. "*Vamonos,* don Roberto—let's get out of here!"

The Messerschmitt continued descending; a deathly-black shadow raced along the ground in its wake. Suddenly, the plane leveled off to begin a strafing run. "What are you doing?" Oberst White inquired.

With a jerking motion the old bus lumbered back, away from the airport, away from the fuel truck.

The pilot armed the cowling guns and fired a short burst of tracer, incendiary and armor-piercing bullets at the fuel truck. With a loud whooshing sound the fuel truck erupted into a massive, orange and black fireball that reached eighty feet into the sky.

The Messerschmitt executed a tight, low-level turn then banked left to view the destruction. "They're getting away," the pilot exclaimed through clenched teeth.

The bus crawled away in reverse, the flames rolling off the hood and licking the windshield.

"What the hell did you just do?" Oberst White demanded.

"I am eliminating the witnesses, Herr Oberst."

In a panic don Roberto backed the right side of his bus into a ditch, the pleated exit door blocked by the dirt bank. The old engine groaned like a wounded beast and the gears ground loudly as he tried in vain to make the bus move forward.

The Messerschmitt circled, the big inverted V-12 engine still running rough.

Trapped in the bus Miguel cradled Carmen in his arms. Don Roberto struggled with the clutch and gearshift, murmuring an *Ave Maria* under his breath.

The Messerschmitt lined up for a second strafing run at his intended target, the ancient bus.

Carmen, Miguel and don Roberto stared helplessly at the approaching fighter plane through the side windows of the bus. The engine's drone intensified, filling the hollow interior of the bus with dread.

"Miguel," Carmen exclaimed, "I am so sorry. I only wanted to bring you your lunch, and now we will all die!" The baby stirred in her womb.

"Carmen," Miguel cried out, "know always that I love ... You!" He had forsaken his family and fortune for her. Now he would shield her with his body that she and their baby *might* live.

The pilot armed the wing cannons and dropping the nose of his plane ever so slightly, he lined his gun sights up for the kill.

Don Roberto continued praying, "*Señor Dios*, take care of my daughters," and in resignation, he signed himself with the Holy Sign.

"No witnesses!" The pilot screamed savagely.

A crisp, barely discernable metallic click was heard over the engine roar, "*Nein, Oberleutnant!*"

Instantly a dark shadow descended, covering the bus like a funeral shroud and vanishing nearly as quickly as it had come.

"Oberst," the pilot exclaimed, "what are you doing?"

"*Actung*, Oberleutnant! I am holding a cocked and loaded Walthers P-38 pistol to the back of your head. Let those people live, Oberleutnant, the War is over! Or do you wish to start yet another war with the Mexicans? There are just the two of us now. We will not defeat them!"

The Messerschmitt soared over the autobus like the *Angel of Death*. Miguel, still holding Carmen, looked over his right shoulder. "They are leaving, *mi amor*," he managed to say.

"If you shoot me, Oberst, who will fly you to South America?"

"Any schoolboy can fly these Messerschmitts, Oberleutnant, you know that. And if you want to keep flying, fly this bird east, southeast right now."

"But Oberst, that setting will take us straight into enemy territory!"

"Yes, to the lower Rio Grande Valley of Texas. We have to find a desolate location to land, where our aeroplane will not be detected. From there we shall hike to the nearest road."

"Oberst, we will be recognized for what we are, Aryan master race! They will execute us!"

"Fortunately I speak fluent English. If you keep your mouth shut, we will simply be two Americans with engine trouble. There are small airports throughout the Valley. It will be a simple matter to hitchhike to the nearest place where we can purchase some good, high-octane aviation fuel for your aeroplane. Then shall we fly to South America!"

"How far is this Valley, Herr Oberst?"

"Not more than eighty miles by air, if you fly straight, Oberleutnant."

"If we climb to twelve thousand-feet, we can *glide* that far, Oberst."

"No Oberleutnant! Fly fast! Fly low! They have radar at Moore Field in the Valley. There are trainers there. Novice pilots, but good enough and more than eager to shoot your crippled aeroplane down!"

"Herr Oberst," the pilot protested, "I am a veteran combat pilot. I have twenty confirmed kills fighting in the European Theatre. I am not afraid of novice pilots!"

"Confirmed kills against Hurricanes and Spitfires," the Oberst retorted with contempt.

"The Royal Air Force proved to be a formidable enemy of the *Luftwaffe*, Herr Oberst."

"Indeed, men of unquestionable courage in antiquated battle planes with inferior armament. A single hit from your .30-millimeter motor-kannon will blow a Spitfire to smithereens. But tell me, Oberleutnant, have you ever tangled with a North American P-47?"

The pilot hesitated. "Are you questioning my courage, Herr Oberst, or merely my skill as a fighter pilot?"

"I am witness to your courage, Oberleutnant. I have seen your skill attacking targets that do not shoot back. Had I not stopped you, you would have murdered a busload of unarmed civilians. That takes neither skill nor courage!"

"And tell me, Herr Oberst, you have never murdered anyone in the name of the Fatherland, *Ja?*"

The Oberst held his pistol loosely in his right hand and hung his head. "*That is irrelevant, Oberleutnant; the war is over. You and I are men without a country.*"

"I am a German, Herr Oberst. I serve the *Fuehrer* and the Fatherland."

"Ha! The Fuehrer is dead. We are without a Fatherland, and unless you wish to join the Fuehrer as a *dead* Nazi, fly as if the very devil were on our tail!" The Oberst paused for effect.

"The Laredo Army Air Base across the river has a squadron of new P-51 Mustangs. If the Mexican authorities notify the American airbase of your unwarranted attack, we shall learn how skillful you are at fending off an attack by modern battle planes."

"If you had let me execute the witnesses, there would be no one to notify the Americans!"

"And you think that fireball did not call attention to an armed war plane with Nazi markings flying over enemy skies?" *Yes, the fireball ... We are not only men without a country, we are hunted men.* The Oberst realized with a start, *we are ... Dead men!*

"Enemy skies? We are not at war with Mexico?"

"Ha! Berlin failed to notify you Oberleutnant, that you were flying into enemy territory. Mexico declared war against the Axis Powers on June of 1942!" *The Oberleutnant is not only an idiot, he is a homicidal maniac!*

The pilot's eyes widen in stark realization. *The quail was right. They were in hostile territory!*

"And their allies, the Americans, will fly to the assistance of their neighbors to the south, Oberleutnant. The Mexicans do not have reliable warplanes handy, only a handful of AT-6 dive-bombers—a gift from Mr. Roosevelt. They *will* ask the Americans for assistance and the Americans will be more than eager for the chance to score one final kill against the Luftwaffe. All we can do now is run and hide."

* * * *

Within thirty minutes the Messerschmitt glided over the lower Rio Grande Valley of Texas. "Set this bird down," the Oberst commanded, "over there," he gesticulated with the pistol. "In that clearing by those sand dunes …"

"The war *is* over, Oberleutnant. We are men without a … country." The Oberst's blue eyes went blank with resignation. "We are … Dead men …"

The Oberst raised his pistol firmly in his right hand, asserting in his native tongue what he had come to believe of the Nazi ideal: ***Jedem das seine!***

Fear registered in the Oberleutnant's face. He screamed, "Nein Herr Oberst—"

As the Messerschmitt slid into the quicksand the Oberst repeated his final statement, this time in English … ***Each gets what he deserves!***

* * * *

Approximately sixty-two years later: The lower Rio Grande Valley outside of San Benito, Texas …

Rene and Steve drove and stopped right in front of something shiny and metallic protruding from the ground. Staring through the windshield Steve exclaimed, "What the hell is that?"

"Looks like a blade—oh shit! I think I know what that is!"

Hurriedly both men got down and stood around the buried object.

"What the hell *is* that? An old sword, or what?"

Rene tentatively gave the blade a kick. "Solid. It's not just stuck in the ground."

And he walked away from the blade to a point directly behind it. "Look here, Steve."

Rene prodded something metallic buried in the sand with his right boot toe, "I *know* what's buried here," he stated enigmatically.

"It's an airplane, Steve. That blade is part of the propeller sticking up, and this is the top vane of the tail."

Steve gawked at the evidence. Yes, Rene was right. It had to be an airplane.

"Steve, go back to the Blazer and bring a couple of shovels. It doesn't look like … a real big plane."

Frequently chugging water, both men vigorously dug around the downed plane, flinging sand over their shoulders, barely staying ahead of the shifting sand returning to reclaim its prize. "A la madre," Steve suddenly exclaimed. "Look Rene, this mother has big machine guns still attached to the nose and wings!"

"Some kind of battle plane, a fighter I think," Rene asserted nodding once, "but it does not appear to be one of ours …"

"What do you mean?"

Pointing at the right wing Rene added, "See that big cross on the wing Steve? That's a Nazi cross. This is a Nazi fighter."

Steve's jaw dropped, "How the hell did it get *here*?"

"Could have flown up from South America with a belly fuel tank, fueling frequently along the way. Or on a submarine, maybe …"

"Submarine? An enemy sub in American waters?"

"Yeah Steve, now we know that Nazi subs were prowling the Gulf. The Mexican Military actually sunk a couple of them. Little plane like this, they probably just disassembled it and crated it on the deck of a submarine then put it back together on the beach. Boca Chica Beach is deserted most of the time, anyway."

Steve wiped dirt from the double canopy with his right hand, leaned close and cupped his hands around his eyes. He gawked through the opaque glass. For a second his heart skipped a beat. Disbelieving he looked again. Yes, his eyes were *not* deceiving him.

"Rene … You'd better see this."

Rene stared through the opaque glass from his side of the downed plane.

"Do you see them?"

"I see them Steve. Looks like they were riding tandem."

"Is that the pilot in the front?"

"Yes, he's the one with the bullet hole through the back of the head."

"I thought that was a bullet hole." Steve straightened and looked right at his friend. "Do you think the passenger shot him?"

"Must have, he's the one holding the pistol …"

LITERARY NIGHT AT THE LOPEZ BAR

by Mona D. Sizer

The town was going to tear the place down the next day. It must have been nearly a century old. Nothing but cobwebs and dirt held it together. Why not one last hurrah before the final curtain? The idea wasn't as crazy an idea as you might think.

The Lopez Bar had seen its best days when San Benito was a trail town. Not Abilene or Dodge City, of course. Just a convenient wide place in the road at the end of a day's easy drive, as steers meander. Just a stop along the way where the trail hands could get a shot of redeye before they drove their herds to the riverboats in Brownsville. A day or so later, they'd make a stop on the way back to lose their money to whiskey, cards, and dice.

When the railroad finally came to the Valley, in its insolent manner it laid its tracks not a stone's throw from the Lopez Bar while it stole away its business. The cowboys didn't drive steers any longer. Their jobs became their legend. Instead, the cattle were loaded through chutes alongside the rails that ran through the great ranches in Nueces, Kenedy, and Willacy County.

But somehow, the Lopez Bar had managed to hang on, a decaying hulk, its clapboards streaming rust from the broadhead nails. Its oak floors pitted and rotted until the present owner had been forced to throw down some sheets of cheap plywood in front of the bar so customers wouldn't put a foot through the worst spots.

You'd have thought a hurricane might have blown it down by now, or a careless match set it afire, but it had borne a charmed life. For some unknown reason it had survived. Now, in a short twenty-four hours, San Benito's city fathers had scheduled it for demolition. Its contents along with its rotten timbers were to be hauled away.

And so, tonight. A romp. A bit of irony. A delicious joke. A young professor at the University of Texas at Brownsville, had devised a literary festival in a place where all but a few of its past patrons had been content to sign with an "X" and point to the labels on the beer bottles.

Yes! Here we all were that night—a mixed bag of writers and listeners playing a game right out of the '70s—real college professors, poets, novelists, students, dramatists, probably some merely curious strangers who'd wandered in, searching for distraction. It was all pretense. We weren't serious. The best among us just came for a chance to read to a sympathetic audience while we all got drunk on lukewarm Tecate and Carta Blanca.

A gray-haired slattern in a faded, draggle-tailed dress and flip-flops slapped back and forth among the patrons. How long had she waited tables here? In the crackled and smoky mirror behind the bar, her long, straggling hair, sunken eyes, and hollow cheeks passing back and forth looked more like a floating ghost than a real person.

In the unlikely case that anyone was hungry, she had a pot of *menudo* simmering on the antique stove in back. Five pounds of beef tripe with a full head of garlic. It's why chili powder was invented. And beer's the only thing in the world that'll cut the heat and the grease.

So all the patrons that night were drinking their beers as fast as they could take them off the bar and carry them to the booths.

The first of the literati to read that night was a beefy author who had preserved the tale of a lady wrestler called "The Masked Strangler," who dispatched her victims with a death grip of her thighs round their necks. Imagination supplied whether she had jumped them from the front or the back. The final jump ended in the arms of a lover, and we all applauded and cheered.

Second was a woman who instructed us all to chug-a-lug a beer every time she read the word "Santiago." Of course, she managed to inject the name into her deathless prose a couple dozen times in a ten-minute presentation. Since Santiago was a faithless lover who left a lonely madwoman behind him when he rode away, she wandered calling his name for at least a two pages. "Santiago!" she called. "Santiago! Santiago! San-ti-a-go!"

The gaunt barmaid raised her head from where she'd paused for minute behind the bar and stared hard around her. Her hollow eyes glittered in the dim lights. The hint of a smile twisted her mouth.

We were all laughing and getting drunk fast or pretending to. I lifted my can to my lips but didn't drink. Not because I was opposed to alcohol or couldn't stomach the warm beer, but I couldn't imagine myself using the one and only bathroom that opened directly into the bar.

As a consequence I was almost cold sober, and that was the only thing about me that was cold. Smoking was allowed, and the "swamp cooler" over the doorway, while failing to cool, had more than adequately raised the humidity. We would have all died of noxious fumes if the front door hadn't been open onto the street and the windows open toward the railroad tracks.

Like a ragged ghost the gaunt woman flapped in and out among the patrons. The smoke grew denser, the swamp cooler hummed, the single street light developed a rainbow halo as a warm fog rolled in.

It drifted through the open windows lazily curling through the cobwebs stretched between the antlers of a stuffed deer head tilted crazily in one corner. In defiance of the laws of gravity, the fog's skeletal fingers even crept up the dirty walls. It wound itself around the old sombreros, the ragged canteens, and the sweat-darkened troopers' hats hanging crazily on the forest of antlers above the dark mirror with the flaked silver backing.

The old saddle hanging on the wall behind the pool table glowed silvery damp from the shadows. Beneath its coating of dust, dark metal that might have been silver *conchos* winked in the light as the pool players circled the table.

Santiago, the faithless lover, never returned. The madwoman called for him until her voice faded away into the darkness.

The assemblage clapped and stomped their approval of the tale and reached for fresh beers, and the draggle-tailed barmaid flapped among them.

I checked my watch and then lifted my bottle to finish off the beer. As I leaned back, my gaze caught sight of a figure lounging in the shadows at the end of bar. I blinked and passed a hand over my eyes. Sure, he hadn't been there a minute before. A dark man, his face shaded by a black, flat-crowned hat. A stranger. He didn't look as if he belonged in our group. Yet somehow he looked more at ease than we did in the ancient surroundings.

"Who's next?" David called. He rocked back on his heels, obviously more than a little drunk and staggering on the uneven floor. Steadying himself with a hand on the bar, he called, "Tales? *Leyendas?* Dramas? *Vamonos!* This is the first and only literary festival of the Lopez Bar." He chuckled as he raised his beer. "To a short tradition, but a merry one. *Salud!*"

"*Salud!*" a few of us responded.

"Now, who's next?" David called again. "Who'll be part of immortality?"

I couldn't take my eyes off the figure behind him, a substance in the shadows, a watcher from the darkness beneath his hat. All sorts of phantasms rose in my imagination. Despite my distaste for the plumbing, I helped myself to another beer.

The line was long outside the bathroom. I tempered my drinking. Now and again, I slipped a look at the dark figure. I couldn't help the shivery feeling down my spine. Then I noticed that he had a beer sitting in front of him.

With a long exhale, I relaxed. He was just someone out of the night. Simple explanation for everything.

A young grad student stepped forward hesitantly to read a tale of murders at the Santa Margarita crossroads. Replacing innuendo with gore, his earnest rendering was easily as unpleasant in its own way as the story of the Masked Strangler.

Knives flashed. Six-guns boomed. Blood splattered the floor and the walls. The old man fell while his wife ran screaming into the night. The bandits darted after her laughing. Her screams choked off in a hideous gurgle.

No one cheered or stamped when he finished. The Masked Strangler and Santiago had been crowd pleasers. This overwrought attempt at serious writing was merely depressing. The young man looked around him clearly disappointed by the polite applause that died immediately. Everyone turned back to his drinking. In an effort to head off hurt feelings, David slapped him on the back and handed him a consolation beer.

Determined not to let the party be sober long, an old drunk cleared his throat noisily and began to recite. At his first sentence everyone howled with laughter. It was bawdy. It was obscene. The women should have been insulted. But nearing midnight after many a round, the audience was past caring.

Amidst the laughter, the young man turned his back and nursed his beer. No one else seemed inclined to read.

I glanced again at my watch. Three minutes to midnight. Thinking to slip quietly to the door, I set my beer half-finished on a nearby windowsill. As I looked up, the dark figure stepped out from the corner. Hat pulled low over his face, he passed within inches of the disappointed author's slumped shoulders.

The reaction was instant and electric. The writer straightened as if cold steel had touched this skin. He stared hard into the smoky mirror with its cracked and flaking silver. Alarmed, he swung around, looking left, right. What in the world had passed him by?

My imagination was working overtime. Surely, he must see the lithe figure striding down the room toward the pool table. I could see him. Clearly. His dark shirt and vest. Even his hard, sharp chin beneath the hat brim and his straight black hair spreading sleekly over his collar.

The young man shrugged his shoulders uneasily before he turned back to the bar.

As if the fog had dampened all the spirits, the sounds of conversation muted.

Out of the night came the lonely, three-toned whistle of a locomotive. Hoarse. Calling steadily through the night. Calling, calling, calling nearer and nearer, warning unwary travelers off the tracks.

And something else.

The distinct, unmistakable thud of a shod hoof. Pawing. And a whinny that ended in a snort. A horse. Unmistakably, a horse. Impatient to be away.

I glanced at the window. Where was it? Where had it come from? At this time of night?

When I looked back, the dark man had hooked his hand in behind the horn and lifted the dusty saddle down from the wall. Oblivious, the pool players continued their study of the table while one bent to make a shot.

No one except me in that entire assemblage seemed to notice as the man strode back down the room, the saddle slung over his shoulder. Ice cold chills trickled down my spine. No one but me. And the gaunt woman who now stood at the end of bar. She clutched the scarred oak edge in a death grip. He passed her by almost within arm's reach. His boot heels made no sound on the floor, but the old tooled stirrup leather creaked audibly.

Curious beyond fear, I slipped along the wall to follow him. Who was he? Clearly, he'd got what he came for.

Much closer now—its whistle sounded a warning. The train rolled down the track. Strangely, it wasn't a new locomotive at all with three or four bright halogen lights shining for miles down the track and that was odd. It was old. Old as a locomotive from a Western movie. I didn't remember that I'd ever seen one with a revolving headlight sweeping starkly in and out of the bar, lighting the patron's faces as if they were caught in Strobe flashes.

Just as I reached the door, the light blinded me momentarily.

I blinked. By the bit of light spill from the door, I made out a pale horse. Reins looped over its neck, it waited impatiently beside the porch of the Lopez Bar. The dark man tossed the saddle over its back and reached for the cinches. As he tightened them, the train rolled nearer. Its big single light revolved; its wheels clicked and clacked over the old rails.

I stood in the doorway, fascinated, as the dark man swung up into the saddle. He paid me no more mind than if I hadn't been there. I wondered for a moment if he could see me, or did he have no reason to acknowledge me?

Almost as an afterthought, he looked back over his shoulder. He raised two fingers to his hat brim. I blinked. Was he bidding me *adios*? I raised my hand.

He wheeled the horse. It cantered toward the railroad track, just as the train arrived. Alarmed, I stepped out to the edge of the porch. He'd have to rein the animal back. The horse didn't check.

No! Without pause the rider spurred the horse. It leaped forward. Its legs seemed to leave the ground as it sprang in front of the locomotive.

I closed my eyes in horror. Then opened them. The pair had leaped onto the tracks just at the second the train rumbled past. Yet, nothing had happened. No mayhem, no bodies, no blood. No blood at all.

I steadied myself against the porch railing. A coal car followed the ancient engine. Behind it ancient boxcars, cattle cars, rumbling and clacking rolled in front of my eyes. At the end a caboose, dark except for a brakeman's lantern swinging from a hook. A last lighted afterthought.

Shivering, I dropped down off the porch and walked to the tracks. I stooped and passed my hand over the rail where the horseman had crossed. Nothing. No sign and no vibration. Just old, cold steel.

What had I seen? Sick and frightened, I turned back, gritting my teeth to still their chattering.

What I saw behind me raised the hair on the back of my neck.

The ghostly woman stood leaning against the door jamb of the Lopez Bar. Her arms were crossed tight over her meager chest.

In that instant I knew the one he'd saluted.

In the darkness her face glowed pale and strangely young. Her eyes glistened with tears.

* * * *

The literati departed swiftly thereafter. The next day, the demolition crew took less than twelve hours to clear out the contents, demolish the old building, and flatten the earth.

Where it had stood, nothing remained.

And the woman—

I asked David what happened to her. He looked at me with a puzzled expression. "You musta got really drunk. Or else you got your nights mixed." He shrugged. "Don't you remember? We served ourselves."

PERSONAL GHOSTS

by Bertha Zúñiga Campos

Just one hundred years ago, *la frontera*, the border between the Rio Grande Valley and Mexico was still a wild frontier—the last frontier. It was a treacherous place to live or die. And whoever did not die from gunshot could always count on the flu, yellow fever, or malaria to do the job. This once God-forsaken place is home to a multitude of ghosts, and accounts of ghostly apparitions from *la llorona* crying for her drowned children to long-dead soldiers of the Mexican War still guarding old Fort Brown are told and retold to young children growing up in the region.

Everybody has an aunt, uncle, grandfather, or grandmother who picked up a hitchhiker along a cemetery road late at night only to find out it was *la muerte!* Every youngster has been warned never to walk along the banks of a canal after midnight. If he does, he risks encountering the weeping woman who will make him jump into the murky waters in search of the children she drowned!

I don't visit haunted places, and if I happen to spend the night in the old Ringgold Hotel in Rio Grande City, known for its ghostly inhabitants, I don't even think about the specter I might encounter during the night. I sleep very well. Rattling doorknobs, rustling curtains, or clanging water pipes do not frighten me. Strangers long dead, no matter how tragic the circumstances of their demise, do not bother me. I have grown up with their stories and have grown accustomed to sharing my space with them wherever we might be. The ghosts who give me pause are the ones I have known in life. The ghosts I have encountered are personal ghosts. They are the ones who haunt me, bewilder me, and cause me to reflect.

Some of my ethereal friends are former colleagues or former students. A few are relatives I have loved deeply and lost.

My ghosts haunt me, but they do not frighten me. In fact, most of the ghosts I encounter don't linger long. They stop by on their way "out." Some I see only moments before I learn of their deaths. I sense their presence in a passing thought or fleeting memory of some long forgotten time I spent with them. I always wonder what made me think of them. Then, I realize that they were thinking of me and decided to pay me a visit one last time, as if to say, "We never had the chance to get together as we said we would."

I might have said, "Stop in next time you're in town; we'll talk over coffee," and so now they have, but it's too late for talk and they have no need of coffee.

My ghosts remind me that my time on earth is running short. The clock has stopped for them and will stop for me before I get to do the many things I want to do that I keep putting off. Mostly, they remind me that I spend too much time on pettiness. They have come to insist that I cultivate friendships, mend relationships; honor loved ones before I have no time left to do so.

My ghosts remind me of the times I waited too long to pay a visit or make a telephone call or write the letter that would have kept me in touch with them. By the time I sense their presence in the coolness of the morning mist or the quiet solitude of my courtyard at night, it is too late to make the earthly contact, to say "hello," "I'm sorry," or "I really value your friendship." I feel guilty for the words I did not say to them and the times I did not spend with them during their lifetime. Mostly, I am sorry that I did not get to say goodbye. These ghosts are not strangers of bygone days. They have meant something to me, and I am sad that they are gone.

My saddest ghostly encounter occurred the night my father died. He came to my home to look in on us one last time. He had been very ill for one brief week, but no one expected him to die. I was only twenty-eight, and I never had the chance to tell him just how much he meant to me. I had just assumed that he knew how much I loved him. I thought I would have him for a very long time, that there would be time for thanking him for being present at every important milestone of my life.

My dad was my hero and my biggest fan. "SweetPea, you can do it if you try," he'd say. No matter what I proposed, he supported it. I ran for class office every year in high school, and Dad always took time off to come see me give my campaign speeches. He was delighted when I won every year. "I knew you could do it, SweetPea," he'd say. "I knew you could."

I never thought my dad could love anyone more until I married and had my girls. My dad adored his grandbabies. Every day of the week he spent in the hospital, he asked about them and told me to go home to care for them. "I don't want them alone at night, SweetPea. You go home now." And I did.

The night he died, I awoke in the middle of the night and started out of my room. Halfway down the hall, I stopped. I thought I heard voices coming from my girls' room, and I could *feel* his presence in the house. When I came to their bedroom, I stopped frozen in my tracks and stared ahead! I saw him standing in my hallway looking at his grandchildren. I had just left his bedside at the hospital a few hours before. But there he was! He blew a kiss and cast a loving glance at my sleeping children, and then he disappeared. Had he been talking to my girls? Would they wake up from a dream of one last visit from their grandpa? I knew they would. All I could do was whisper, "I love you Daddy," before returning to my room to wait for the hospital to call.

Sure enough, the next morning my six-year-old asked, "Why does Grandpa call you SweetPea?"

Some of the ghosts I know have been students. Samantha, a pretty former student of mine disappeared about two miles from her home. She was never seen again, alive or dead. Samantha was a pretty blonde girl in my sophomore English class. Her father was a local farmer. She was shy and very quiet in my class. During Teacher Appreciation Week, Samantha surprised me with a corsage. None of my students had given me anything, and I could hear giggles when she shyly handed it to me. I accepted it with a genuine thrill, especially because it was given so sincerely.

Although Samantha was a bright girl, college was not in her plans. By her senior year, she had married her high school sweetheart. In personality, he was the exact opposite. Gregarious and handsome, he was the football hero all the cheerleaders wanted. But Samantha got him, and it was evident that he was crazy about her, though it was rumored that he had a slightly jealous streak. They married right out of high school, and he went to work on her father's farm. She worked in an office in a neighboring town.

Life seemed to go well for them until the day she placed one last phone call to him before her disappearance. She told him she would be working late but would be home before dark. He never saw her again.

I found myself thinking about her a few days before I learned about her disappearance. I had not seen Samantha for at least ten years, and I wondered why she so suddenly came into my thoughts. I remember feeling overcome by sadness the day she slipped into my memory. If I had known her better, I might have picked up the phone to call to see if everything was all right. The thought of her nagged me. I felt as if I should do something, but not knowing what, I pushed her from my mind.

When I learned of her disappearance, a cold, icy feeling spread through me. I had the most horrible feeling, a sort of knowing, that she was dead and that she simply wanted to say, "Good-bye."

Though her body has never been found, Samantha's spirit steals into my memory every now and then, a sweet, lost young woman. How I wish there were something I could do to help her.

Kevin was another one of my students who paid me a visit from beyond the grave. Kevin was a prankster—a likeable kid, who always had a smile on his face. Tall and lanky, he always wore boots, faded jeans, and a cowboy hat. We called kids like him "kickers" in those days. He loved country-western music and chewing tobacco. Kevin was fond of me, but he was not fond of school. He kept his watch synchronized to school time just so he could be the first one to leave at the end of the period. Every day, he rose from his desk exactly thirteen seconds to the bell and walked to the door counting down as he went. The bell always rang just as he reached for the doorknob. It never failed. Kevin kept his watch so synchronized that his peers began putting their books away by his timepiece.

During spring break of his junior year, Kevin drank too much beer and drowned in the Arroyo Colorado. On the day he died, I was at work in my classroom, taking advantage of the quiet before the students returned from break. The door opened and shut. The bell rang. I looked outside, and a faint breeze stirred the leaves of the oak tree outside my window. I looked at my watch and smiling, thought of Kevin, not knowing yet that he was dead.

I continued teaching in Room 6205 for the next fifteen years. Every now and then, Kevin paid me a visit. He made sure I felt his presence during quiet times, so there would be no mistaking he was there. Once, as my students were finishing a final exam, the door swung open and shut and the bell rang. Smiling as I thought of Kevin, I told them, "It's just the Ghost of Room 6205 reminding you it's time to leave."

The last time Kevin paid me a visit was the week I retired from teaching. I was alone, grading papers in my classroom. Quitting time came around, and then the door, opened—shut.

"Time to go home, Ma'am."

"Goodbye, Kevin," I whispered.

My personal ghosts make me aware of the web of life. I may have come into this life alone, but I live it in community with others, entangled by ties of family and friendship and work. They slip into my memory every now and then. I notice them in the rustle of wind through leaves on a quiet morning or in the stillness of my courtyard at midnight. I say a prayer for them; they are souls in purgatory now, no need to be afraid. They are only looking out for me, assuring me perhaps that crossing over is not as bad as some would think.

SHIFT CHANGE

by Judy Stevens

"Git Out!"

Lillian couldn't fault the old man for shouting. After all, he had Alzheimer's—and there was a ghost in his room. Soon enough, the disease would capture this new delusion, and he'd smile sweetly again, and then things would return to normal in this wing of the nursing home, where memory drifted into oblivion. She eased into the chair at the nurses' station and grimaced as she glanced down the dimly-lit corridor and its orderly march of doors to the very last one. She had left his door wide open, and had even turned on a night light, but nothing seemed to help. She gave a light sigh of resignation: it looked like those muffled shouts would become the selected music for tonight.

Lillian barely noticed the age spots on the back of her hands as she flipped the chart open with the ease of one who gave no quarter to advancing years. She made a few careful notations then paused, her eyes focusing again on the doors. She thought of Marta's half-serious remark, that in the late hours of night these benign doors became creepy portals to the spirit world. Lillian also saw them as portals, but in another sense: beyond their blankness lies an unknown realm of once-independent souls, now trapped in the prison of their minds.

This insight had from the first evoked a nurturing spirit within her. Now, as she reflected on it, she knew she wouldn't retire this year. How could she turn her back on these souls she had loved in a way she could never quite express? How could she abandon her calling? All those years of skinned knees and schoolyard sniffles, of patching godawful wounds in M.A.S.H. units, and of making endless rounds in hospitals, had been but prelude to this place, where bodies needing diligent care lingered long past the death of their minds. As morbid as this seemed to others, here was a place she could finally call home. Here she was useful; here she was essential; here she came alive. Leaving here would mean a small death.

"One chart done," Lillian thought. "Making good time." Her thoughts drifted past these simple notations on paper to the woman they represented, sleeping peacefully beyond that half-open door. In just a few hours this sweet soul would undergo a bizarre transformation, becoming a living whirlwind just in time to greet the day staff as they shuffled in with the dawn.

Lillian admired their courage, but they thought her braver—to face a ghost at night.

"Git Out!"

Anger laced the old man's feeble shout, causing Lillian to release a ragged sigh. She knew the doctor meant well when he said to check in at intervals but otherwise let the patient vent, but to Lillian it was like letting a sick baby cry. Her thoughts strayed back to the first day she welcomed that whisper of a man stepping shakily from the active wing of the nursing home, her heart aching at the sheer loneliness peeking through the tissue of his bravado. In the other wing, where people moved around with purpose, he had outlived everyone who had ever cared to visit him, growing older and older—so old in fact, that everyone started calling him "Father Time." Over here, he became everyone's darling, scooting around in his walker, trying to pinch nurses' rear ends. Then he broke his hip and forgot how to walk. And now he was confined to bed, waiting for the inevitable—whose unspoken name was known by all.

The last two nights had been a major challenge to Lillian's nerves, ever since Father Time had noticed a ghost in his room. But at least he had an excuse for his delusion, not like those who otherwise should have behaved with professional skepticism. It both bemused and aggravated Lillian, who only desired to treat the man with dignity, even if it meant letting him face the figment of his fading imagination. It didn't matter that no one else had seen it: no one else was supposed to—the story went—unless they were going to die. But everyone agreed on one thing. The "Lady in Black", who had been camped out in Father Time's room seemed to be having trouble beckoning Father Time to follow her away to death.

Everyone knew the story of the "Lady in Black." It was one of the most enduring of the ghost stories told here in the Valley. Lillian took each ghostly tale with a large grain of salt, for it seemed wherever there were nurses and doctors and patients and death, there were spirits and hauntings and bumps in the night. Lillian had long ago learned to humor everyone and nod her head knowingly and leave it at that. She knew that if you believed in all the rumors and superstitions and stories that came from every hospital and nursing home, then you'd be sure to believe in cherubic phantom nuns ministering to grateful patients in the middle of the night when pain envelops every pore. You'd also believe in cold hands brushing nurses' necks while they were sitting at their stations charting, in phantoms walking the halls, looking for their dying kin, and in day birds who sang at night and the buildings they perched on creaking and settling just before a death. And, if you truly believed in all these things, then you were ready to believe that whoever saw that shadowy figure of a woman shrouded in black was next to die.

To Lillian, all these tales were mere embellishments of a far greater wonder: the wonder of what happens during and after death. That curiosity originally led her to this job and was the reason she loved it. That reason was still there. Though she had witnessed death many times, never had she glimpsed its true reality. Maybe that was why she had grown weary of the endless speculations and superstitious meanderings that attempted to explain this unknown. And that is probably why she rather liked the simple reasoning of a kindly doctor who once said that perhaps these events were remnants of thought left behind by those who passed away.

"Git out! Dimmit—git ooouuut! Oooooooouuuuuutttt!"

Lillian stood up and glanced longingly at her unfinished stack of charts. Then—stiffly at first—she walked down the hall past door after open door until she reached Father Time's room. She gazed at the small bony figure illumined by the beam of light from the open doorway. He had flung his covers off again. Thank goodness the railings were still up so he couldn't fall. Two wild eyes and a shriveled hand stabbed the air in her direction.

"Doncha come near me! Go away!"

Lillian forced a reassuring smile. This was getting serious. She mulled over what else the doctor had told her: that she was authorized to give the patient a sedative, if she chose. In all her years as a nurse, Lillian had never sedated a patient just to quiet things down, but the level of downright—terror—in the old man's eyes disturbed her. He might actually hurt himself if this went on. She studied the man a moment more, then made her decision.

In no time at all the light sedative drove the wild look from Father Time's eyes. As Lillian took his pulse, he gave a faint sneer and slight nod to the door behind her, then dropped into deep, restful sleep. Lillian covered him with his blanket and turned to leave, then paused at the door, shivering in the icy draft, wondering if one blanket had been enough. She dimmed the light and made a mental note to notify maintenance to adjust the air conditioning.

As she eased back into her chair at the nurses' station, Lillian decided to be honest with herself about working too hard at her age, and made a decision to slow down. Tomorrow night would be her last shift for several days; and as much as she loved her work, it was time for a change of pace—maybe part-time.

She smiled. The kids had even surprised her with a stay at South Padre Island and made her buy a swimsuit and promise to get it wet. How could she refuse an offer like that?

Lillian's contented mood lasted until the morning shift change, when Marta pressed into her hand a special protective talisman that she'd gotten at the Espirituista Curandero, and wouldn't let Lillian leave until she had promised to carry it whenever she went near Father Time. Lillian shrugged inwardly and thanked her and put the token in her pocket, chalking it up to the fact that tonight there would be a full moon.

As she drove back to work that evening Lillian thought again of all the tales she'd heard over the years about ghostly happenings in even the newest hospitals and nursing homes in the Valley, and decided if these tales were true, the population of spirits had surpassed the living, so the only logical thing to do was to step up production in the maternity wards just to catch up.

If that tale of the Lady in Black was so blasted true, then why on earth was Father Time still alive? Did the Lady make a mistake and get the wrong address? To think of being stood up on your deathbed, Lillian thought wryly, as she settled into her station for the night.

"Meds all checked, charts clear for now, making good time," she thought. A full moon usually touched off those with dementia, but for some reason all was quiet tonight. In fact, you could hear the wall clock ticking. "The calm before the storm," she thought, remembering the time they got two admissions in the middle of the shift. Then she realized how unusually quiet it was in Father Time's room. Marta said you don't even know they're dying, but the lady in black—she does.

Lillian reviewed Father Time's chart: no reactions to the sedative she administered last night. Nothing in the day chart about condition change. In fact, he had made small improvements; even moved his legs a little. Incredible. Everything normal. Maybe tonight would return to normal, too. She gazed down the corridor.

Unless …

Something in the pit of her stomach reminded Lillian of the one thing she hated about this job. If Father Time had lasted one more night, someone else would have all the paperwork and notification procedures to handle. But now, if the pit of her stomach was right, it meant she had the lucky draw. She sighed and pushed herself out of the chair and stood up straight. As if that purposeful movement would erase the inevitable, she walked down the corridor.

The meager light from the hall told nothing about the figure sprawled on the bed. So small, so frail, so—quiet. She couldn't see the chestwall from here. Was he still breathing? She tiptoed in, taking her stethoscope from around her neck and warming it, then gingerly touched his chest above his heart, fearing the worst.

"Nurse?"

Anyone else would have jumped in fright, but Lillian just stared openmouthed in confusion. Gone from Father Time were the monotones and bland face of late-stage Alzheimer's. In its place, wry humor and a knowing smile crinkled his face and animated his eyes. Lillian shut her mouth and tried a weak smile to help her wake up from this insane dream.

"She's gone, is all I got t' say," Father Time said matter-of-factly. Grabbing the covers and rolling over he added, "She exchanged me fer someone else." Then, a muffled: "G-night."

This was no hallucination. This was real, and this was something Lillian had never encountered before. Unease chased wonderment as Lillian's mind tried to wrap around the implications of what had just happened, and all the charting, the questions, the medical probing facing this poor old man. Her hand wrapped around something in her pocket. It was Marta's talisman. A grin spread over her face. Questions be damned! She'd be his talisman; she'd be talisman to them all.

Father Time began to snore lightly. It looked like he'd live another thousand years. Lillian glanced at her watch. One hour left till shift change, then all hell will break loose. She might have to cancel that trip to Padre Island.

A movement in the mirror startled her, but a lifetime of facing death helped her shake off rising terror and the urge to flee. She looked closer, then grimaced. It figured. All this and now having to call the exterminator. She unceremoniously ended the life of the small intruder, washed her hands and quietly left the room, and the door—the portal to this new, unknown world—ajar. As she walked back to her station, Lillian peeked in every door, half expecting another terrified face staring at a ghost in the corner, but everyone still slept like babies.

The full moon gave the central nurses' station an ethereal glow, intensifying Lillian's melancholy mood as she realized Father Time no longer belonged here, and would be sent back to the other wing. She wondered if his loneliness had been restored along with his thoughts? Would anyone bother to notice his loneliness in a place where everyone moved around with a purpose? But none of that mattered now. It was all out of her hands.

Still—if his intellect failed again, and he came back here, she knew that somehow she would be waiting to welcome him as before.

Lillian found his chart, opened it, and made as professional a notation as she could under the circumstances, hoping her colleagues and the doctors wouldn't think her gone mad. Then she stretched and sat back, and gave a weary sigh to it all. She reached in her pocket for the talisman, then realized she had left it in Father Time's room.

Suddenly, like an icy draft, the immensity of life and death and unexplained healing made Lillian shiver. She closed her eyes and gave another, more ragged sigh, as she felt the real fear that been haunting her all these years—the fear that her retirement would lead her back to this corridor, to live the rest of her life unaware, beyond one of these blank doors.

She shivered again and opened her eyes.

Before her stood a woman shrouded in black, beckoning her to follow.

IN THE MUSEUM

by Janet R. Wilder

Michelle tried not to think about it. She just wanted to do her job. The work was boring and lonely, but the pay was excellent and she needed the cash. She wiggled her shoulders to rid herself of the creepy feeling and proceeded to add the next entry into the computer spread sheet. Settling into a routine, she was disturbed yet again by the draft that convulsed her in a bone-chilling, seaweed-stinking paroxysm of shivering. She stood up to check the window knowing as she crossed the floor that the window was shut. She had checked it only a few minutes before.

She was freezing cold and, at the same time, damp with perspiration. "This is impossible" she said aloud, but it was not her imagination. This was her third night. She couldn't have imagined it *every* night—several times each night.

Saving her work on the computer, she stepped out of the office and into the hallway, hopeful that she'd find an open window or door somewhere in the dark museum that would account for the draft. Having done this drill before, the search for doors and windows was evolving into a routine. This would have to be the last search but she hoped that the diversion would clear the air in the office of the seaweed infused chill. She suppressed a small, involuntary shiver from her sense-memory of cold, rotten seaweed. Maybe there was a problem with the air ducts. Yeah! That was it! The air ducts!

Seventeen year-old Michelle Peña was a senior at Port Isabel High School. She was an excellent student, accepted to attend UT Austin in the Fall as a history major. Her family had lived in Port Isabel for several generations, so the opportunity to earn some college money by transcribing catalog cards into the computer of the Museums of Port Isabel was like a miracle. Michelle had spent many happy afternoons at the museum's discovery lab with her family. She was proud of the lighthouse and of how the history of the Champion family, who had owned the general store building that now housed the museum, was intertwined with her own. The museum director had given her a key and the code for the alarm system at the historical museum so that she could work at night. She would be able to get her homework done, have supper with her family before going to work and still have her weekends free. Initially, she had been enchanted with the idea of being alone in the museum. Initially.

Returning to her desk, she began to type. She was quite involved when someone touched her right shoulder. She stopped typing and turned around. No one was there. Had she imagined it? She checked her watch. She had an hour before she could leave. Turning back to the keyboard, scanning the lines on the card, she picked up and began to type. She completed five more cards when she felt someone touch her shoulder again.

Pat, pat, pat.

Michelle froze. This time she was certain it was not her imagining anything. Her knees were so shaky she didn't think she could stand, but she did. She turned knowing she'd find the room empty. It was. Reaching behind her for the chair, she sat down.

She thought about the pat, pat, pat. It wasn't a *tap*, like someone wanting her attention. It was closer to a *there, there now!* gesture—almost as though someone was trying to calm her, to tell her "don't be afraid". She entered a few more cards, but with a corner of her mind waiting for the stinky cold or a pat on the shoulder, she found herself making mistakes. "I'm just tired, is all", she thought. When her time was over she locked up and drove the few blocks to her home. The lights were on, her family cheerfully greeted her. Her mom had made her a snack of a glass of milk and a pumpkin empañada. It was worth those three hours of typing each night for Mom's after-work snacks. Michelle considered telling her mother about the strange things that happened in the lonely museum, but sitting in the brightly lit kitchen, eating a yummy empañada, she felt slightly silly. She was sure that her *over-ripe imagination*, a tag she bore from a year with a doting English teacher, was at fault.

Friday night at the museum was quiet. No cold air. No taps on the shoulder. Michelle was sure she had imagined the goings on of the previous three nights.

She finished her transcriptions with no interruptions and drove home singing with the radio, happy to be free for the weekend.

Tuesday evening found Michelle at the computer in a cheerful mood. She didn't have a steady boyfriend but Tony Ramirez had asked her to the prom and she had quickly accepted. It was hard to concentrate when thoughts of prom dresses, limousines and the good-looking Tony in a tuxedo were bouncing through her head. She hummed softly to herself as she copied the cards onto the spread sheet. Type, type, type, tab; type, type, type, tab; the rhythm of her fingers matching the rhythms of an imagined dance with Tony playing in her head.

Her peace was suddenly broken by the thunderous crash and clatter of shattering china. She thought she'd jumped a foot out of her chair only to find that she was still seated. The sound came again. Clatter! Crash! The clammor echoed through the empty halls. There was no mistake. Dishes were being broken in the museum.

Michelle was a smart girl. If there was an intruder in the museum, she didn't want to confront him. She clicked *save* and shut down the computer. Then she walked to the door, checked that it was closed and turned off the light. She sat down on the floor in the darkest corner of the office. If someone was meaning to rob the place, they wouldn't see her. She'd be safe. The dishes clattered and crashed again. Michelle made herself very small and squeezed even closer into the corner. Her back was tight up against the wall when the almost forgotten hand of Thursday night pat, pat, patted her on her right shoulder. There was no way anyone could reach her shoulder! No one could possibly be standing behind her, yet—there it was again—pat, pat, pat ... *there, there now, don't be afraid.* Strangely, it calmed her.

Michelle sat in the corner for what seemed like years. She hadn't heard anything besides the air conditioning system for a while. She was deciding whether or not to get up and investigate when—pat, pat, pat ... *it'll be all right* ... the comforting hand patted her right shoulder. She got up and switched on the light.

Mr. Mendoza, the museum director, had shown her the alarm system. She checked it. None of the lights was flashing which meant that no doors or windows had been breached. "Maybe a shelf fell down", she thought. She stopped to listen one more time. Finding nothing but silence, she went into the hall and turned on the lights. She checked all of the exhibit rooms and nothing was amiss. She checked the storage areas. Nothing broken. Not a shard of pottery out of place. Not a sliver of crockery disturbed. The display of china that might have been sold in the Champion's store was untouched. She knew what she'd heard, but there was nothing she could see that would have caused the unmistakable sound of dishes being smashed.

It was time to leave so she went back to the office to get her things. She stepped into the office and was slammed in the face with icy-cold air and the stench of rotten seaweed. She gasped, recovered her breath, grabbed her backpack and sweater and lit out, stopping just long enough to arm the alarm system. She ran to her car, climbed in, locked the doors and sat for a while. She was shaking so hard that she had to hold tight to the steering wheel or she'd surely shatter into a million little pieces. Slowly regaining her composure she almost wished for the pat, pat, pat of the comforting, but unseen, hand.

That evening, Michelle turned down her mother's proffered after-work snack. She went straight to bed where she curled up under the covers and felt safe. It took her a while to fall asleep, but when she did, she dreamed of Tony and the prom dress she'd be wearing.

In the darkness of the Port Isabel historical museum, the soul of Jeffrey Champion wandered. It was a tortured soul; one that knew no peace. The presence of young women with long dark hair upset him. When he was upset, Jeffrey liked to throw the china his father sold in the general store at the walls. The sound of it crashing and smashing into a million smithereens made him feel good. The fact that it cost his father money made him feel even better. Jeffrey Champion was very, very angry. He was so angry that even though he had died in 1920, he was still throwing dishes at the walls in 2006.

Charles Champion had come to Port Isabel in 1897. As a young soldier from Indiana, he had done a tour of duty at Fort Brown where he met his wife Matilda at a church gathering. Using his mustering-out pay and her dowry, the Champions built a general store with an apartment for themselves and the family they hoped to build. They had two children, but the little girl had died when she was quite small and only Jeffrey survived into adulthood.

Matilda thought she must have eaten too much spicy food when she was carrying Jeffrey. That was how she accounted for Jeffrey's constant anger. For as long as she could remember, Jeffrey and Charles could not agree. When Charles decided to train one of Jeffrey's school-mates to assist him in the general store,

Jeffrey, though he wanted nothing to do with commerce, was furious. It broke her heart, but Matilda counseled her son to leave the Rio Grande Valley and find a career that agreed with him. Jeffery joined the Army and fought in the World War I trenches of Europe. He'd had a lungful of mustard gas which only increased his anger.

After he returned from Europe, Jeffrey stayed at home. Only through the careful maneuvering of Matilda did he avoid confronting his father. Then he fell in love. Sarita, with her long, dark hair, was the most beautiful woman Jeffrey had ever seen. She was kind. She was loving. He felt happy and calm when he was with her. He wanted nothing so much as to marry Sarita and live a long and happy life together. Charles would not countenance his son marrying a "Mexican" and promptly disinherited him. Jeffrey didn't care. He got a job on a shrimp boat owned by one of Sarita's uncles. He could make his own living despite his father's prejudice, but Jeffrey never forgave his father for the slight to his beloved.

Jeffrey married Sarita Peña on April 13, 1920. For the first time in his life, he knew how it felt to not be angry.

In September of that year, Jeffrey was out on the Gulf in the shrimp boat when a hurricane arose. Jeffrey's vessel sank. All hands were lost. In November, his body washed up on South Padre Island. It was severely decomposed and covered with rotting seaweed. He was identified by the inscription on his wedding ring. There would be no long and happy life with Sarita.

Sarita was heartbroken. She was a good woman and she knew that Jeffrey's mother, Matilda, would be grieving for her only child. Though she regretted leaving her many nieces and nephews, Sarita went to the apartment behind the general store and comforted her mother-in-law. Sarita didn't speak much English and Matilda didn't speak much Spanish.

Sarita never remarried. Matilda lived and grieved for another fifty years. Sarita spent all day, every day, comforting her mother-in-law without words. She stood behind Matilda's chair, patting her on the right shoulder—uno, dos, tres—*there, there, there.*

ECHOES OF PALO ALTO

by Nelly Venselaar

Can you hear the soldiers marching?
Through the fields of Palo Alto
Hear the guns ablazing

Deafening noise of cannons.
Armies marching in rhythm
Striding relentlessly forward.

Forging ahead toward unseen enemies
Hidden yet behind the ridge of mesquite and bush
The cavalry is advancing.

The sky is darkening
They still march on
A haunting anxiety in the air.

Following General Taylor's proud, white steed
The troops march on
Steadily onward.

Major Ringgold on his dark brown mount
Keeping the foot soldiers
Advancing onto the battlefield.

What thoughts were in their minds
While they were walking, walking?
Did they see glory and victory?

Or suffering and death upon meeting
The enemy with cannon and sabers?
Or did they see themselves in the Great Beyond?

Determinedly they go on, notwithstanding
The shell and shrapnel damage
Until the enemy is defeated and victory is won.

Now
All that's heard are the echoes
Of the marching troops of Palo Alto.

THE HANGING ROOM

by Ann Greenfield

Edinburg, Texas, May 2, 2006

Today is the anniversary of the only execution to take place in the Hidalgo County Jail. All week I've heard noises. Maybe I'm being paranoid, but I'm not the only one who has had strange things happen to them. Other docents and staff members have heard noises at the old jail. Some have seen the ghost.

"It's just an ordinary day, a day like any other day," I reassured myself, as I pulled into the parking lot of the historical museum. The clock on my pearl pathfinder read 9:15. It was quite dark. The moon hung low in the eastern sky.

The tour starts in fifteen minutes, I'd better hurry. I'm not sure I'm ready for today. I hope nothing happens.

I stumbled on the curb, dropped my keys, and spilled my coffee.

Calm down! You're acting like a superstitious idiot!

I pulled open the mesquite door to the grand lobby and felt a coolness to my skin. It contrasted with the heat and humidity of the Rio Grande Valley night, and soothed my irritation at my own clumsiness.

It's too quiet. Last tour of the evening. Thank God we'll be finished before eleven. I don't want to be here at eleven.

I walked through the main corridor out to the patio and stopped at the bricks branded by ranch logos. I lingered over the family names of McAllen, Guerra, and Bentsen.

I'll ask the archivist if he has heard or seen anything today.

I opened the glass door to the old jail and walked into silence. I heard my exhalation in the stillness. The air was thick with anticipation. Mike gave me a nod and cracked the window in the Margaret McAllen Archives.

"Hi, Mike," I said breaking the quiet. "Have you heard or seen anything today?"

He rolled his eyes and shook his head no. *Of course he hadn't heard noises. Mike didn't believe in ghosts. Why would he? He was an historian.*

"What's wrong with your voice? You sound hoarse," commented Mike.

I couldn't tell him I was a little bit nervous.

"Have you got a cold?"

"Maybe," I croaked.

OK! Well, I'm glad Mike's here anyway. I don't want to be alone in the jail. Especially today!

I shook my head and walked toward the original stairway. *What would Ortiz have been thinking on this day in 1913?*

Reluctantly, I climbed nine narrow stairs that lead to the jail tower and the hanging room. I hugged the gray railing for support careful not to touch the original walls.

My legs are shaky. I wanted to hold on to the walls, but that was a no, no. Years of rising damp had deteriorated the masonry brick and mortar.

A shadow danced in the doorway of the hanging room. A dark shadow. It filled the room. I held my breath.

Was the shadow my imagination? Was someone up here?

"I don't believe in ghosts." I said out loud. No one was listening.

"Hello," I called. "Mike?"

Had he taken the main stairway?

I stifled a scream.

I wanted to bolt! You're fine I told myself.

I climbed the remaining six metal steps to the second floor. I peered left around the corner into the main exhibit room.

Nothing!

I quickly glanced right toward the maximum security cell.

Nothing!

I kissed the cross on my necklace and headed to the gallows room.

Cold penetrated the front of my chest. I gasped for air.

Am I having a heart attack?

I grabbed my chest and tried to catch my breath. My heart was pounding. I leaned on the railing that surrounded the trap door. I heard the sound of wood creaking beneath heavy footsteps. Then, a slight nudge between my shoulder blades pushed me forward, pushed me on to the trap door.

Oh My God! Is someone there?

I snapped my head around. My eyes widened! A dark shadow washed over me! I was momentarily blinded. A silhouette stopped in the center of the gallows door.

Did I hear chimes, one, two …?

Clang!

I jumped.

Did I wet my pants?

The echo was deafening. The silhouette was sucked through the floor and disappeared. A shiver ricocheted along each vertebrae and radiated to the tips of my fingers. My heart now throbbed in my throat and I had to take deep breaths to calm myself.

I looked around. Nothing but silence!

Was this how Ortiz felt? Today is the anniversary of the hanging, the only execution to take place in the Hidalgo County jail. I knew the story.

Hidalgo, Texas, February 1912

The streets of Hidalgo were dirt, and dust rose with every horse drawn buggy and wagon. Irritated by the blistering heat, Domingo Gonzalez and Abrám Ortiz quenched their thirst in the town square. The open air café gave them a view of the Sunday market as they gulped *cerveza* and ate *barbacoa*. Shoppers came across the Rio Grande from Reynosa to buy fresh produce and dry goods.

One couple in particular caught the eye of Abrám. The man was simply dressed, but carried an air about him. Abrám watched them squeeze grapefruit and cantaloupe. They bought several bags of goods from the market spending more money than Abrám had seen in his lifetime.

Martín Martinez had a beautiful young woman on his arm. Abrám ogled her every move. Florencia held a blue and yellow dress close to her body and twirled laughing. Martín grabbed her by the waist and pulled her close to him. She giggled. Ortiz was excited by her coquettish smile. Martín kissed her on the cheek. Abrám noticed her wine-colored lips.

Gonzalez ordered another round.

With a swig of beer, Ortiz elbowed his friend, "*Mira*, look! She's beautiful, *verdad?*"

Gonzalez nodded his head, "Holy Mother of God. It's true. Very beautiful!"

Florencia stood on tiptoes and whispered in Martín's ear. The more Florencia laughed, the more lustful Abrám became. He swallowed the last of his beer, nodded toward the young couple, and stood. They followed Martín and Florencia toward Mexico.

Their attack was swift and brutal. Martín was blind-sided by a club to the back of his head, kicked, and beaten while his beloved wife watched. He never knew when Abrám's knife plunged between his ribs into his heart.

Horrified, Florencia's tongue froze in her throat and rendered her mute. Fruits and vegetables bounced into the tall grass and were left to rot in the searing Valley sun, the blue and yellow dress splayed on the path.

Hands! Hands!

Hands were all over her, inside her dress, covering her mouth, fondling her breasts, between her legs. The ground was hard and a sharp pain was burning inside her. The smell of beer filled her nostrils and their laughter rang in her ears. Gonzalez held her down, pinching and suckling her nipples; Ortiz thrust again and again. They took turns until they were satisfied.

Florencia tried to fight, but their strength overpowered her small stature. Tears streamed down her face into her bloody hair. Eyes fixed on Martín, she saw the tattoo.

Ortiz forced her to watch as he cut off Martín's finger for his silver wedding ring. He forced Florencia to place the bloody ring on his finger.

Gonzalez frisked Martín for valuables and found his great grandfather's gold pocket watch and three dollars in change.

Florencia knelt beside her husband and prayed he wasn't dead. She stared at the men as they fought over Martín's possessions.

"The boots are mine," said Gonzalez.

Ortiz narrowed his dark eyes. He gritted his teeth. "You have boots. These are my size. I'm taking them."

Gonzalez started to object, but Ortiz held up the bloodied knife. He dropped the hand-tooled leather boots and walked over to Florencia. "What about the woman?"

Florencia tried to stand, but Gonzalez grabbed her by the hair and restrained her.

Ortiz pointed at Florencia and shrugged. "You can have the woman. I'm finished with her."

Florencia wondered what he meant. She was afraid for her life.

Gonzalez waved, *"Adios, amigo."*

He dragged Florencia to his home. He threatened to beat her to death like her husband if she resisted.

Florencia was a clever woman. She gained the trust of her attacker by cooking meals and washing clothes and being agreeable. She asked, "If I'm going to be your wife, what's you name?"

Domingo Gonzalez was tricked into believing she was content. Florencia became friendly with the wives of the other ranch hands. Oralia, one of the wives, confided to her that her brother Abrám and Domingo were lifelong friends, inseparable, and that they often went to the market in Hidalgo for supplies.

"Does your brother have a tattoo on his forearm?" asked Florencia. "A *mariposa*, a red butterfly?"

"Yes, why do you ask?" said Oralia.

Florencia shrugged. "I met him once with Domingo, but I can't remember his name."

"He's Abrám Ortiz," said Oralia.

Finally, Florencia knew the names and whereabouts of her assailants. At the first opportunity she escaped and immediately informed the Hidalgo County Sheriff, Anderson Baker. A warrant was issued for Abrám Ortiz and Domingo Gonzalez.

The trial of Abrám Ortiz began on Wednesday, April 3, 1912, two months after the attack. Florencia was the star witness. She pointed a finger at Ortiz. Fury erupted from her lips. No longer able to contain herself, she screamed, "It was him! He's the one who killed my husband! He raped me. It was him. He's the one!"

Ortiz protested, "I'm innocent. I've never seen this woman."

"That's my husband's wedding ring," Florencia seethed.

The jury foreman, A. A. Kelly, and eleven jurors individually signed the verdict:

"We the jury, find the defendant Abrám Ortiz, guilty of the crime of murder in the first degree as charged in the indictment, and fix his sentence as death."

By April 3, 1913, all appeals were exhausted. One year later the sentence for Abrám Ortiz was pronounced: "To be hanged by the neck until dead."

Hidalgo County Jail, Edinburg, Texas, Friday, May 2, 1913

Anticipation was in the air. Some families left Edinburg to protect their children. Others came from neighboring towns for the hanging. A crowd gathered around the opened jail doors. Florencia stood in the front row.

Sheriff Baker shackled the legs of Abrám Ortiz and tied his hands behind him. He escorted Ortiz to the gallows. Ortiz stopped at the entrance. He looked at the unfamiliar faces gathered around the railing to witness his hanging; deputies, prominent townsfolk, the doctor, even a priest. He didn't know a single person in the gallery. No one came to support him. Not one person came to say good bye. He felt all alone.

The noose dangled from a brass ring embedded in a mesquite beam two stories above the trap door. Sheriff Baker pushed Ortiz between his shoulder blades onto the gallows door. The noose was secured around his neck. Last rites were offered and last words were given.

"There is no heaven for me, Padre," he declared. "Only hell."

Florencia heard the venomous laugh of the man who killed her beloved Martín. It would be the last time.

Ortiz spat vicious words to the gallery, "She's a *puta*, a whore. I'm innocent. I'll come back from the grave. I'll haunt you 'till my name is cleared. You'll never be rid of me. I'll meet you in hell. You can kill me, but not my ghost. *Lo malo, no muere.* Evil never dies."

A black, cotton hood dropped over his head. The courthouse clock struck eleven. Hipolito "Polo" Jackson voluntarily pulled the leaver.

Clang!

The sound was deafening as the trap door was sprung. The sandbag weight attached to the door to ensure opening thudded against the west wall. Ortiz gave an audible gasp as he plummeted to within a few feet of the ground floor. His neck snapped. The crowd was silent. The grating sound of the swinging gallows' door reverberated throughout the town square.

Ortiz was pronounced dead and placed in a wooden coffin. Volunteers backed a single, horse drawn wagon up to the jail house door and loaded the coffin. A grave was dug on land donated from the Gonzalez Ranch. Abrám Ortiz was buried on Doolittle Road in the small cemetery east of town. No words were said. No marker was placed.

Justice was served for Florencia and her husband Martín Martinez.

Edinburg, Texas, May 2, 2006

Chimes rang from St. Joseph the Worker Church as I left the museum. A pale, full moon floated in and out of scudding clouds. *My mind isn't playing tricks on me. All week I have heard noises. I'm not paranoid!* This was the anniversary of the hanging, the only execution to take place in the Hidalgo County jail. True to his words, Abrám Ortiz was haunting the old jail, the last place of his earthly existence. The bells tolled ... nine, ten, eleven.

Today is the first time I saw his ghost.

Author's note: Domingo Gonzalez, also know by the name Concepçion Bueno, fled to Mexico. After the death of Abrám Ortiz, he was arrested in Cameron County, tried for an earlier murder, and served a life sentence.

Part III

▼

Restless Spirits

ONE HOT NIGHT IN SOUTH TEXAS

by Janice Workman

The party was in full swing!

The Celebration of Nothing Special was the holiday declared by all spirits to be their favorite. This year's theme: Come As You Were.

"What are you up to these days, Mary?" I asked the tall, dark-haired, fair skinned woman at my side.

She was sipping a vodka Martini, straight up, with a twist. "Because olives look too much like eyes," she told the bartender with a wink in my direction.

"Oh, it's summer break, so I have the chance to be home. I was getting a little tired of the dorms. 'Bloody Mary, Bloody Mary' every weekend! Those girls don't even get it right. I'm not materializing for anyone unless she turns her back to the mirror. I don't care how many rum and cokes they've had."

"Who's the band tonight?"

"Elvis. Unless he has another rush job in the Bahamas. He's been getting some pretty regular sightings there lately. I hear he wanted to take some time off to work on his music though. He's been shifting some of the focus by appearing as John."

"John?"

"Yes, you know, Lennon. But John isn't into parties, so you won't be seeing him tonight. Besides, he's hanging out at some sort of Beatles reunion thing all week."

"Thanks for the scoop. I'm going to mingle. Later?"

"Maybe, but only if you turn your back to the mirror." She vanished leaving a fall of red dust.

I stopped by the buffet and helped myself to lady fingers, dripping in cherry glaze, and some sort of green goop that looked straight out of Ghost Busters, but tasted a whole lot like lime Jell-O.

"Have you seen Casper?" I asked a trio of figures, drifting by like bleached bed sheets.

"He's over in the corner, sulking," one of them offered. "Poor boy. Just found out he's fallen from the Saturday morning lineup."

"Oh, the fickleness of fame." I heard a male voice mutter drolly. Looking up I stared into the Adam's apple of the headless horseman. His head, tucked underneath his arm, blinked at me and smiled. "I know exactly what he means. Every few years it's a remake of the Sleepy Hollow thing. Other than that, I've been pretty much retired. But I predict they'll discover one of these days that it's hard to find talent like mine with a good head on his shoulders, and I'll be back in the saddle again."

"Good luck!" a gravelly voice rasped behind me. "I've been trying for a comeback for years now, but find myself in the same old bit parts."

"Marley!" I exclaimed, turning to clasp his hand. "It's been a while."

"Yes, good to see you too," Marley said, slapping me on the back, his chains jingling. "Other than December, I don't get out much. Even then I'm stuck with Scrooge and the three stooges. A few times scriptwriters have tried to leave me out all together, but I persuaded them, if you know what I mean." He produced a loud pathetic moan and clanked his chains so loudly he attracted the attention of some others standing around.

"Hey, I didn't know there was going to be a talent contest," a slender blond in pink taffeta and a letterman's sweater called to us, blue eyes twinkling as she joined the conversation.

Marley's old eyes glowed lecherously. Plucking a glass of champagne from a near-by tray, I made introductions.

"Marley, this is Charlene." I gestured to our newest ghost; I mean guest. "Charlene, Marley."

"Nice to meet you, call me Char." She simpered, offering a cool hand adorned with a wrist corsage. "I can't stay long," she apologized. "I promised the guy who lent me his sweater and gave me a ride over here that I would get it back to him by midnight."

She looked around inquiringly. "Have you seen Mary? She promised to show me some make-up tricks and give me the name of a new vanishing cream she discovered."

"Sweet girl," said Marley, as she floated off, leaving the scent of roses in her wake. He yawned and moaned again. "Think I'll see if I can chase me up some decent ale, this champagne just doesn't cut it."

Just then the band broke into a loud rendition of "Cry, Cry Baby". Janis tossed her hair, threw back her head and howled the vocals, but a gorgeous spirit materializing by my side distracted my attention.

"Why do they ask her to do that every year?" she asked, with down-turned ruby lips, shaking her silky black hair from moist eyes with a sigh. "It was fine once or twice or three times even. Now it's just old."

"I don't think I've had the pleasure." I said, touching her slender arm.

"My name is Isabella, but everyone calls me *Llorona*." At my quizzical glance, she sighed and dabbed at her eyes with a handkerchief. "Look, it's a long, sad story and I don't want to get into it now, okay? I'm going to check out the food."

"Sure, no problem. It was nice to meet you." I let it go at that. It was a party after all, and I didn't want my ignorance to spoil the evening.

Mary glided close, smiling over the rim of her glass, "So I see you met our *Llorona*. Don't think twice about it, she's always been that way. One sideways glance and she turns on the water works."

Moments later, security rushed by me to quell a disturbance created by the *chupacabra* and his vampire sidekick trying to crash the party. Sparks flew and sulfur filled the air until they were vanquished.

"They try that every year," a tall, stately gentleman informed me, appearing suddenly in front of me, top hat in hand.

"I know you! You're Honest—"

"My friends know better and just call me Linc," he interrupted with a grin. "Nice party. I was delighted when I heard they secured the old morgue building for tonight. I wouldn't be caught dead in a theater."

"And graveyards are so passé," Mary interjected.

I chuckled, nodded in agreement and took a sip of champagne.

"If you'll excuse me, it seems I'm needed in Washington." As he began to fade, he grinned. "Apparently my presence is required to sway a vote."

"Party's over," Marley called from across the room. "There are live ones headed this way with those electronic contraptions they use to 'discover' us."

"Those things don't really work, do they?" I asked. "Geraldo had a whole program about Ghostbusters and all he got was static."

"Well, it's real enough to keep them coming back and writing books about it." Marley grumbled. "I'm not interested in sticking around and becoming another chapter for some ghost hunter wanna-be."

"Now, Marley, calm down." Mary said soothingly, as she scanned the room, noting other spirits were becoming restless. "This is part of tonight's entertainment."

"What? You actually invited them?" Marley asked, incredulously. "Why on earth …"

Just then the thunder of hoof beats could be heard, pounding across the UTB Commons. A bugle echoed in the distance followed by a single word, "Charge!"

"Mary, tell me you didn't." Marley roared with delight.

"Didn't what?" I asked, confused.

"She called in the cavalry!"

EL DIA DE LOS MUERTOS

by Robin Cate

Who calls us from this graveyard?
Is it the voice of a young boy
filled with exuberance
and a pocket full of pay day?
This boy who jumped
from one boiling sugar vat
to another and missing his mark,
landed in the boil.
Did he die still smiling at his own bravery?

Who calls us from these graves?
Is it the voice of a child who left too soon?
Mamá's little angel and *Papá's* little man.
A child so delightful that when he died,
his *Mamá* followed him into a twin grave
and *Papá* never smiled again.

What of these unmarked graves?
Are they from the families:
Martinez, Rodriguez, Garcia?

Listen to the sounds of these names
Calling from the graves:
Hernandez, Gutierrez, Perez.

And, what will call you from your own grave?
Will you die from exuberance?
Will you die from a broken heart
because someone left too soon?
Will death come the ordinary way
of age, of disease, of boredom?
Who will yell from your grave:
He was a risk taker!
She was *Mamá's* little angel!
He was *Papá's* little man!
Will we be placed in unmarked graves
and return as skeletons riding bicycles
wearing flowered hats
rattling our bones
and singing *canteras?*

THE HOUSE WHO COULDN'T LET GO

by Eileen Mattei

"Wake up! The kitchen's flooded again," Joe yelled in the pre-dawn dimness. "I'm going to turn the water off."

I tumbled out of bed, grabbed the mop and towels and fell into the routine, grumbling about all the good it did having the plumber here to fix things up only two days ago. I was wringing out towels when Joe sloshed past me with a ladder. He punched holes in the ceiling with a screwdriver to let the accumulated water drain through before the weight collapsed the sheetrock. While I kept mopping up, he headed to the attic to put a patch on the latest piece of aged copper pipe that had sprung a leak

Over breakfast, we listed the string of mini-disasters that had assaulted us in the past month. It started with the irrigation well breaking on our 35th anniversary, the day we decided to move out of our too-big-for-two-people house. That was quickly fixed and quickly forgotten because within a week, we had found the perfect cottage to grow old in. We forked over the down payment the next day before leaving the Valley on a long-awaited trip to Seattle. Airport delays gave us time to make little lists of the painting and pruning we could do to make the old house attractive to buyers.

But home again, looking out the kitchen windows to the patio, we sensed something had changed drastically: we couldn't see the patio for the trees. The ancient and massive mesquite tree which shaded the north side of the house had toppled across the full length of the patio. Joe bought a chainsaw to cut it up. Hauling it off took days that we had planned to spend painting and primping.

The next week, air conditioner servicemen swarmed over the house checking the three units and giving them a positive prognosis: old but running fine. The painters were patching and priming the living room ceiling the next morning, while I tried to concentrate on an article with an approaching deadline. When the sound of running water penetrated my concentration, I headed to the kitchen to turn off the faucet and found a waterfall sheeting down from the flourescent fixture. I ran for the main cut-off valve and dashed back to sweep the water off the tile floor and out the back door as the cascade slowed to a trickle.

I longed for my preferred response to domestic challenge: when in trouble, when in doubt, run in circles, scream and shout.

Instead, I went into the attic to pinpoint the leak, but couldn't locate it, partly because the water had sprayed so high and wide. Joe came home in response to my call, and we crawled into the attic's sweltering August heat to find the source of our new headache. Even after tearing up the attic floorboards in the suspect area, hauling out sodden insulation and mopping the pools of water, we were puzzled. Where was the hole? Then a spray of water hit my back. The supposedly healthy air conditioner's water line was shooting a 25 foot stream from a thumb-sized hole in a rude baptism. I choked off the flow with my palm, wishing I had my hands on those air conditioner guys.

So the next morning, when Joe found the kitchen flooded again, our house troubles had passed from the "Oh rats" stage to the "So bad, it's funny" level. Not funny in a ha-ha way, given the cost of plumbers and a/c repairmen.

Funny weird, you know.

"Do you think the house doesn't want us to go?" I asked Joe.

"It could seem that way, but it's just too many years of good luck catching up with us."

"Not always good luck, sweetie. Remember when we came back after that month in Egypt? We walked in, dropped our bags, and the big painting crashed to the floor. That slow leak had soaked and crumbled the entire wall. What a welcome home that was!"

"Right. Like our return from the Panama Canal cruise to that bathroom leak. It may have been a mess, but there was no real damage."

"Do you see a pattern here, Joe? We go away, then we get leaks. The house doesn't like us to go away. And it knows what's coming."

"You have the plumber's cell phone number. Tell him to come replace all the copper water lines. Copper pipes in the Valley just don't last."

Well, Sammy the plumber couldn't get his crew to the house for a week, but in the meantime I discovered the neighborhood bee swarm had taken up residence in the eaves near the balcony I was trying to paint. Joe finally got rid of the 10-comb hive after ripping off some of the upstairs siding ... which meant putting on new siding and paint.

Just before the plumbers came, I woke from a dream that was startling in its clarity and its message. All those leaks ... the house was crying. It didn't want us to go. It didn't want to be left alone. It wasn't angry, just scared.

On one level it made sense: we had filled this spacious, comfortable home with laughter and love, friends, family, and parties, quiet moments and good food, music and happiness. In the 13 years since we'd bought this house from the estate of a retired diplomat, we had often grinned from the sheer pleasure of owning such a light-bathed, welcoming homestead, circled by windows looking onto a tropical paradise of bougainvillea, hibiscus and exotic palms. Even repairmen and delivery men felt compelled to voice their appreciation with variations of "What a beautiful house."

An unhappy house was beyond my scope so I turned to Google for help. A search for house spirits led me to Indonesia and Thailand sites. I became intrigued, my rusty anthropology degree rising to the action like a kite to a good wind. Villages in a tropical river valley in central Java had for millennia honored house spirits with small airy spirit houses. Regular offerings of rice wine, set in front of the little houses, compensated the spirits for watching over the inhabitants, bringing peace and blessings. That didn't seem so far-fetched to me. In Cameroon as a Peace Corps volunteer, I had neighbors whose strong beliefs in the spirits of inanimate objects—thunder and water—had led me to accept that believing does make things so. Some events defy rational explanations.

Sure, it was fascinating information, but how did an Indonesian house spirit apply to me? And what could I do about it? The image of the house crying remained in my head, but I let the matter rest as Sammy and the crew settled in for three days of re-plumbing the house. On day two, he summoned me to the attic to look at a wire. "I was moving the pipe, and this wire next to it just fell apart," the plumber's helper told me, as the security alarm beeped incessantly. The alarm system was disabled, but I could live without it, and, besides, the plumbing job was nearly completed.

Finally the painters returned to tackle the kitchen ceiling. Late that afternoon, the younger painter asked me to come to the kitchen. The far corner of the ceiling had suddenly begun to drip water.

I could only shake my head and think, *It's still crying.*

Joe and a friend went to the attic, found another collapsed air conditioner water line and began making plans to replace it. The painters left me with a bit of paint to finish the corner when it dried out. I abandoned my work and walked to my neighbor's house for consolation and a glass of wine.

"Grace, I really believe the house is crying. What I don't understand is why it is acting like an Indonesian house spirit. It's not mean. It's just sad."

"I remember Jack Desmond, who owned the house before you, spent most of his foreign service career in Southeast Asia," she said, stroking her cat. "The house had so many unusual artifacts, and I think many came from Indonesia. Things like puppets and miniature houses. It was so tragic when he drowned while fishing. The house was empty for six months getting the estate settled."

And the house spirit was left alone with no one to watch over, I said to myself.

I picked up two bottles of rice wine at HEB the next morning. I poured a glass for myself and put some in a saké cup which I placed on a high shelf in the kitchen. "We will not leave you alone," I said out loud. "We will only move out when the next family is ready to move in."

The house went on the market a week later. For the third couple who saw it, it was love at first sight. They signed a contract the next day and wanted to move in with their three kids as soon as we could move out.

Three weeks later, when all the papers had been signed, they stood in the doorway while Joe and I stood on the front walk, exchanging ownership and best wishes. I had just shaken hands with the grinning couple when I saw a single drop of moisture roll from the roof to land on my outstretched hand. I lifted my hand to my face and smelled the faint tartness of rice wine. I turned away, and another drop fell on my hand because now it was my turn to cry.

THE GHOST DIALED 911

by Mona D. Sizer

FADE IN:

INT. WESLACO POLICE DEPARTMENT—911 OFFICE

MAGGIE SANCHEZ (35) sits at her console lazily filing a fingernail. She SIGHS and yawns. She stares at the microphone in front of her, then glances up at the red neon digital clock on the wall.

INSERT: 3:38

Suddenly, MAGGIE sits up alert as information flashes across the screen of console. She picks up the microphone.

                MAGGIE
This is 911.

She listens a minute, then switches on the speaker. The voice of AGENT OLIVIA HERNANDEZ (24), Rookie Border Patrol Officer, blares out in the room that is empty except for Maggie.

OLIVIA (OFF SCREEN)
(gasping, choking)
Agent down! Agent down!

MAGGIE
Repeat, please. Repeat.

OLIVIA (O.S.)
(gasping for air)
Shots fired. Repeat. Shots fired. Agent down.

Maggie presses the emergency button on her desk.

MAGGIE
Duty officer. I need someone ASAP.

SERGEANT CHARLES CLARK (30), senior police officer on duty, answers.

CLARK (O.S.)
You authorizing that, Maggie?

MAGGIE
Yes. Buzzing you in.

CLARK
(enters)
What's happening?

OLIVIA (O.S.)
(screaming)
Agent down! Sandy! Sandy!

CLARK
(to Maggie)
What's her location?

                    MAGGIE
              (shaking head)
        She's using a cell phone. No location.

                    CLARK
        Agent! Can you switch to your radio?

                    OLIVIA (O.S.)
        No. I can't see. It's pitch black.

                    CLARK
        Give us your location.

He gestures to Maggie who slides him a pad and pen.

                    OLIVIA (O.S.)
              (weaker)
        Can't. Too tired. Can't see.

                    MAGGIE
              (tilting console)
        I'm reading her number. 956-555-2309. No name.

                    CLARK
        Damn. What's your name, Agent? Where are you?

                    OLIVIA (O.S.)
        Agent Olivia Hernandez. By the river. Ooh. I'm gonna be sick.

Her voice grows weaker.

                    CLARK
              (to Maggie)
        Border Patrol.
              (to Olivia)
        Suck it up, Agent! It's a big river. Location! Damn it!

                    OLIVIA (O.S.)
               (hesitating, then stronger)
          Santa Ana. By the canoes.

                    CLARK
               (to Maggie)
          What in hell is she talking about?

                    MAGGIE
          The wild life refuge on the river. They have canoe trips.
               (to Olivia)
          Are you where they put the canoes in the water? Or where they
          take them out?

                    OLIVIA (O.S.)
          Don't know. They were using canoes.

                    CLARK
          Who?

                    OLIVIA (O.S.)
          A couple of coyotes with illegals.

                    MAGGIE
          The spots are four miles apart. I'm calling the refuge emergency
          number. Someone can meet the cars at the gate.

                    CLARK
          Call the Border Patrol. Send them up river. We'll meet on the bank.

MAGGIE runs through a list, dials a number. She turns away from Clark to make the calls.

                    CLARK
               (to Olivia)
          Hang on, Agent Hernandez. I'll put out a call to all units in the
          area. We'll run without sirens until we come in. Have you got a
          light you can flash?

                    OLIVIA (O.S.)
                (sob in voice)
I can't move.

                    CLARK
Are you shot?

                    OLIVIA (O.S.)
I-I don't think so.

                    CLARK
Where's your Super?

                    OLIVIA (O.S.)
He was in the boat.

                    CLARK
The patrol boat? Is it sunk?

                    OLIVIA (O.S.)
No. We were hi-jacked. We saw some people trying to cross. Looked like some were drowning. We pulled over to render aid. Sandy was dragged over the side. He went under. (whimpers) When he came up, they shot him.

                    CLARK
God! Sandy Valenzuela?

                    OLIVIA
Yeah. When he came up.

                    CLARK
                (to Maggie)
Instruct Dispatch. All units in the area. Rendezvous at the entry gate to Santa Ana Wildlife Refuge. Emergency.

                    (to Olivia)
Hang on, Agent. Twelve to fifteen minutes. We'll use sirens in the refuge. Signal if you can.

                    OLIVIA (O.S.)
All right.

                    CLARK
                    (to Maggie)
Keep her talking. She sounds pretty desperate.

                    MAGGIE
Will do.

Clark exits.

                    MAGGIE
Hold on, Olivia. I've sent the message to Dispatch. The units will be moving in seconds. Do you need an ambulance?
          (beat)
Olivia! Agent Hernandez!

                    OLIVIA (O.S.)
T-thank you. I-I don't know what's happening. I feel funny.

                    MAGGIE
          (calmly)
You're traumatized and exhausted. You wouldn't be human if you didn't feel funny.

                    OLIVIA (O.S.)
There was a man in a canoe. And people holding onto the sides. A woman, two—I don't know how many—There were little kids, I think.

                    MAGGIE
And Sandy went for the kids.

                    OLIVIA (O.S.)
                (weeping)
            Right. He would.

Maggie glances at the clock.

INSERT: 3:48

                    MAGGIE
            If an officer's in the immediate area, listen for his siren. He
            might be rolling up to the barrier. If there's no one there, they'll
            go on in ahead with the siren.

                    OLIVIA (O.S.)
            I can't hear anything. Not even the river.

                    MAGGIE
            The Rio Grande's a quiet river. Did you have to swim far?

                    OLIVIA (O.S.)
            I don't remember.

                    MAGGIE
            Most places in the Rio Grande this time of year, you can almost
            stand up. Did you try to stand?

                    OLIVIA (O.S.)
            I I don't think so. It happened so fast.

                    MAGGIE
            Can you hear sirens?

                    OLIVIA (O.S.)
            No.

Maggie glances at the clock.

INSERT: 3:50

MAGGIE
(conversationally)
Olivia, do you have family in the Valley?

OLIVIA (O.S.)
(sobs)
My baby girl. My grandmother's keeping her for me. Teresa.

MAGGIE
How old?

OLIVIA (O.S.)
Two. Her-her birthday's next Friday.

MAGGIE
(hurriedly)
Invite me to the party. I love little girls' birthday parties.

OLIVIA (O.S.)
Mi abuela. (My grandmother) She's planned everything. P-pink cake and candles. I've got her presents in the back of my car.

Olivia starts to CRY.

MAGGIE
Stop that. When they bring you back, I'll help carry in the presents. As Clark says, "Suck it up, Agent."

She glances at the clock.

INSERT: 3:55

CLARK (O.S.)
We're at the gate. Nobody's here. Raise the barrier. Maggie, where's this damn canoe ramp?

                             MAGGIE
Go left once you get to the nature center. There's a way to get
up from the river that they could use. I don't—

                             CLARK (O.S.)
Hold it. Here comes a civilian now. Turn on the sirens.

SIRENS begin to wail immediately in the background. One, then two.

                             CLARK (O.S.)
                          (yelling)
                    Get in! Get in!

Car doors SLAM.

                             MAGGIE
Hear that, Olivia. They're coming in! Can you signal? Scream!
Anything!

                             OLIVIA (O.S.)
I can't hear anything! I can't see anything.

The wail of sirens fills the room.

                             MAGGIE
Hear them! Hear them!

INSERT: 4:00

                             OLIVIA (O.S.)
                          (whispering)
I can hear them now. On the cell phone. Not—Are they at
Santa Ana?

                             MAGGIE
They're there, Olivia. Clark couldn't make a mistake. He's the
best. And he's mad. Olivia. You don't want to get in his way
when he's mad. (chuckles) You'll see.

OLIVIA (O.S.)
(very weak)
I don't hear anything except you. I can't move.

MAGGIE
Olivia, stay with me. Do you hear me? Stay with me!

OLIVIA (O.S.)
My baby. My Teresa. Tell her—

MAGGIE
Olivia! Olivia!

The line is dead. Maggie frantically tries other keys. The SIRENS stop suddenly.

MAGGIE
Clark! Clark!

CLARK (O.S.)
We're covering the bank. Did she tell you her location?

MAGGIE
No. And she's not answering. Where are you?

CLARK (O.S.)
We're at the canoe ramp. She's not here.

MAGGIE
She's got to be.
(beat)
She's got to be.

CLARK (O.S.)
We've got the floodlights down on the landing. We're finding tracks. Here's where they came in all right. Beached canoes. Hey! There they are! They're running.

CLARK (O.S.)
Halt! Alto! Alto! O dispiro! (Stop! Or I'll fire!) Son-of-a-bitch!

Maggie listens intently. Two SHOTS fired. (O.S.) Muffled SOUNDS of struggle. Unintelligible CURSES.

CLARK (O.S.)
Where is she? Where's the agent?

Muffled conversation.

MAGGIE
(desperately)
She's got to be there.

CLARK (O.S.)
Hold on.
(beat)
Maggie, I'm sorry.

MAGGIE
(quietly)
Where is she?

CLARK (O.S.)
We're going to have to drag the damn river. The coyote says she fell in too. Son-of-a-bitch probably threw her in.

MAGGIE
But—

CLARK
He had her cell phone. He dropped her cell phone on the bank. Her number's taped to the back. It's her personal. Not issued. She bought the minutes.

                    MAGGIE
               (agitated)
          I talked to her. You talked to her.

                    CLARK (O.S.)
          Looks like her minutes ran out.

Maggie looks at the clock

INSERT: 4:05

FADE OUT.

THE END

HOW GRANDPA GOT WEIRD

by C. Dean Andersson

How'd I get weird? You heard your mom talking.

When she was a little girl she had her school friends kind of scared of me because she'd say things like, "I'm so very sorry," then a dramatic sigh, "but you'll have to <u>excuse</u> Dad. He's a little <u>weird</u>." I suspect she was also a little proud that I was different. No one else's dad wrote books about weird things. Made her feel special. Never has admitted it to me, though. A little game we still play.

Let me tell you how Grandpa got weird.

When I was a kid a little younger than you, we moved to the Rio Grande Valley. I'll show you on a map later. The location matters. You'll see.

One Sunday morning a couple of weeks before Halloween I saw a special ad on the movie page in the local newspaper. Movies changed twice a week in those days, plus special matinees for kids on Saturday afternoon. On Sunday I always checked to see if a western, science fiction, or horror film was coming.

The special ad announced Professor Nightmare's Mid-Nite Monster Show Revue, coming for one night only to the Arcadia Theater downtown. The monster show would be sandwiched between two old horror movies I'd already seen on TV.

Oh! The wondrous things that ad promised. Satan's Blood Burial! Monsters Terrify Screaming Victims! A Man Buried Alive in Person! Regurgitating Reptilian Horrors! Not to mention that Hugo the Killer Zombie was to be set loose in the audience! The Chasm of Spasms was to spawn Ghosts and Ghouls to drag someone from the audience into a Tomb of Terror! And one of the drawings showed a victim strapped to a table while a grinning mad doctor held a big sharp knife poised to slash.

Seeing the ad, my spirits soared, then crashed back to Earth. My folks would never let me go. It was on Wednesday night, a school night. I was sunk. But I was also desperate. So I devised a plan.

I acted like I hadn't noticed the ad, waited a day, then Monday evening told my folks the monster show was the talk of everyone at school. Not a lie. I also said all my friends' parents had said they could go, which <u>might</u> have been true by then, because we'd all agreed to ask by telling our folks the same thing.

Miracle of miracles, your great grandparents, John and Mernie, who were usually pretty strict about such things, shocked me by saying almost immediately that, okay, I could go, as long as they drove me and my friends to the theater downtown and I called for a pickup the minute the monster show was over. No staying for the second feature.

The ploy worked for my friends, too. I suspect now our parents were all in cahoots, giving us a Halloween Treat to remember.

In the two days leading up to That Night, our imaginations and speculations added more and more to the promises in the ad. Sure, down deep we figured it was mostly a bunch of hooey, like the horror movie posters that always promised more than the movies delivered. But hoping some small part would be true made the wait intensely delicious.

The Arcadia was an old place with a big stage in front of the screen where live acts could perform. But it was more than a theater to me. It was a Temple of Dreams, ornately decorated inside and out with high, arching ceilings and, far above, rows of chandeliers hanging down. I loved how it felt to anticipate what I was about to see, sitting in the indoor twilight, the light fading as they darkened the vast cavern of an auditorium for the movie to begin.

We had a ball at the monster show. We didn't notice how the costumes had seen better days or how tired the actors looked under their indifferently applied makeup, playing one more small town venue yet one more time. That realization came later, and I wrote about it in my monster show book. I'll show you sometime.

No, during the show we saw exactly what we wanted to see. Glorious Monsters Galore! And when they momentarily turned out all the lights at the end as the monsters lumbered into the audience, we all screamed long and loud, laughing in between shrieks.

Then it was over. The lights came up. The curtain across the stage was closed. Because we hadn't been given permission to stay for the second feature, it was time to call home and leave. And we did. But I desperately wanted more.

That's why, I'll always believe, after the show I was open to Possibilities, kind of called to them, maybe, and before dawn those Possibilities came to call.

I awoke from a nightmare. I don't remember much about it except the ending. People made of ashes were disappearing into my wallpaper. If you touched them, they crumbled into dust that clung to your hands like greasy black gloves. But as the nightmare faded and my heart slowed its wild thumping, I noticed something worse than the nightmare.

My room was wrong. Backwards. The window had switched to the opposite wall from where it had been. So had the door.

I was too frightened to move for a while; but when I finally did move the room snapped back into place. What a relief! So I rolled over and looked out the now properly positioned window.

It was a cool October night so the window was closed. But I had raised the blinds before going to sleep. A bright moon was out. I always liked how moonlight changed ordinary things, gave them soft edges, blue and mysterious. I looked into our big back yard at the tall old tree on the far side by the fence and at the regulation sized basketball goal Dad had erected for me the year before. Then something out there moved and I froze.

Breath caught in my throat. My heart pounded.

Something was moving dark and low to the ground. Not a dog or cat. Too big. And it moved wrong, flitted along in sudden jerks and starts like a lizard.

Then it was beneath my window, reared up, and looked at me with glowing red eyes.

Seconds stretched out while we looked at each other, both surprised, I think, and those moments of fear and wonder stayed with me all my life.

Though terrified and afraid to move, I began to question what it was. The dark shape of its head was dog-like. Maybe it <u>was</u> just a dog. The eyes shining like red coals could be a reflection somehow. But a moment later that faint hope was shattered.

Without warning, for a heartbeat the backyard was bathed in bright light and I saw what looked in at me. The face was dog-like, yes, but more. Other.

Strings of drool dripped from long fangs. Huge round eyes glowed with red light from within. Big pointed ears were set high on sides of its head. And its skin was hairless, marred here and there by dark splotches. All this I saw in the second the backyard was lighted. Then the instant of light ended. The moonlit night returned. I expected thunder but none came.

The thing at my window looked up at the sky then whipped around with its back to me.

Light came again but not like lightning. It swept across the backyard as if a big spotlight were being held above the house. And this time it stayed on, daylight that was so out of place in the middle of the night that it frightened me more than the creature. But in that light I saw the thing had a row of spines down its hairless back. Then it leaped high, going straight up on what I saw were hind legs like a kangaroo's. It came down on the far side of the backyard and leaped again, straight to the top of the tall tree over there, where it perched like a bird in spite of the fact that it should have been too heavy to do that.

Then it leaped a third time, down from the tree on the other side of our backyard fence just as the light overhead went out and stayed out.

Without thinking I jumped up and ran to the back door. I fumbled with it, my hands shaking. A rational part of my mind told me *no-no-no-do not go out there*, but a need too strong to ignore urged *hurry-hurry-hurry!*

Then I was out there, in the moonlight, looking up for whatever had shined the light. I saw the moon, of course, and a few bright stars, but nothing unusual in the sky. The backyard was its normal self again except for a strange smell hanging faintly in the air. I hurried back inside, but quietly so as not to wake my folks. I put on my house slippers, got a flashlight from the kitchen, and went back out. I used the light to look for tracks in the soft dirt under my window, but I didn't find any.

I stayed out a while, thinking, wondering, but the autumn night was too cool to stay there for long, so I went back to bed. I didn't sleep, though. How could I after what had happened?

After dawn I went to the backyard again. Looked again for tracks. Again found none. And I looked for any other sign that I had not dreamed the whole thing. For that's what I had started to believe. It was the only thing that made sense. But I knew better.

Common sense had nothing to do it. Something impossible had happened. The world was so much more than what I'd believed. I felt like I did in the Arcadia before a movie began, anticipating a future filled with wonders beyond anything I'd imagined might be real.

And I guess you could say that that's when Grandpa got weird, because that's when I started taking unexplained things seriously and looking for answers.

In the local library I found books that helped get me started. I discovered right away I was not alone. Many people had experienced all kinds of things science could not explain. The first book I read was Frank Edwards' <u>Stranger than Science</u>. Then came Charles Fort's <u>The Book of the Damned,</u> Edward Ruppelt's <u>The Report on Unidentified Flying Objects,</u> and more.

And yes, I eventually discovered a name for what I'd seen in the backyard that night, because a lot of other people had seen it too and still do, all over North and South America, and often in the Rio Grande Valley. See? I told you the location was important. There's a town called Zapata down there on the border with Mexico that has even held festivals in the creature's honor, complete with custom made T-shirts and tacos bearing the critter's name.

It's *El Chupacabra*. In English the name means "goat sucker." Its favorite food is the blood of goats. When they're around it's like they're not. They rarely arouse guard dogs. They never leave tracks. Those who've seen them describe pretty much what I saw. One witness claimed the one he watched never touched the ground, that it flew, wings buzzing like a bumble bee while it hovered and sucked a goat dry. Which is pretty bizarre but would explain the lack of tracks. Some wonder, however, if they're not more ghost than animal, or even an antigravity teleportation machine from a flying saucer. But maybe they're from another dimension and only visit the Earth for food. No one knows. Yet.

But someday, someone will find out more, maybe discover a dead one or capture a live one, even make one a pet, though I doubt that'll happen unless *El Chupacabra* or whoever's in charge of them decides to cooperate.

Hey, maybe you'll be the one who discovers their secret. Why not? I've kept all the books I've studied and written, and they're all yours if you want them. But you've got to be weird enough to deserve them, see?

Don't laugh. Go for it, kid. You've got it in you. Just play your cards right and someday maybe your mom will say, "I'm so sorry," then heave a resigned sigh, "but you'll have to excuse my son. He's like his grandpa. A little weird."

But deep down she'll be proud.

CURANDERA

by Georgia Tuxbury

Every night I dream about Uncle Robbie, a man who was killed in a car accident twenty-five years ago. I was only four at the time. In my dream he is kneeling on the floor next to the bathtub where I—a little girl with long, blonde hair—am immersed in bubbles.

There is nothing more to the dream, and yet I awaken with fear running a jagged path inside me. Evil that I cannot discern is hiding there. I strain to see the faces, but the harder I try, the quicker they flake away.

I attempt to box the dream and seal it but it will not be contained. I must lay it out in the middle of the night and dissect it organ by organ. I can neither find the heart to see what makes it tick nor the lungs to find out how it takes in air. Yet it beats and breathes and digs its heels into my fragile psyche.

At first the dream merely toyed with me. I was able to shake it off like a loose briar. Now this innocent appearing dream has snagged me. Fearing it, I have become an insomniac. The effects of sleeplessness and this unshakable fear have eroded my mind.

It is affecting my job. Several times I have been called on the carpet for day-dreaming, an especially serious habit for a nurse in the hospital's intensive care unit.

Even more serious is what it is doing to the relationship with my family, driving Barry, my husband, and Jennifer, my five year old daughter, away from me. They know nothing except that I have lost my sense of humor ... my delight for life. I have hidden the seriousness of my depression from them as well as the cause. When I am home, I sit in my bedroom and try to make sense out of the dream, as if getting to the meaning of it will clear my mind. I tell them I have a headache. Barry has had to act as both father and mother to Jennifer, and I do not relish the exclusion.

There was a time when I played dual roles, too. I chose to be a single mother, selecting a father neither by love nor lust but by genetic résumé. I laughed about being part of the modern family—mother, donor and child—until I gave birth to Jennifer. I tried to make us into a cohesive group, but we were dough without yeast. How I longed for the traditional family. Then I met Barry who loved us both, who filled us in and made us complete.

Barry, working days, comes home in the late afternoon when I take my shift at the hospital. It is such a perfect arrangement. Now, when my life is being turned around, I develop this strange fixation with a dark and deadly dream that could ruin everything for me. I cannot let that happen. I must seek professional help.

I choose Dr. Beatrice Bianca as a therapist since she is well known for dealing with sexual abuse, and I suspect this is the bone that refuses burial. I tell her about my dream and she asks me about Uncle Robbie.

"He lived with us for several years after Mother divorced Dad. I remember very little about him except what my mother told me."

"Yes?"

"Robbie was her favorite brother. She had four. He was the best looking. The most fun."

"What about your experiences with him? Can you separate them from your mother's memories?"

I try. But my recollections are like a melding of clouds where a vague image of a tall man in Western hat and boots wavers in and out. Not a glimmer of personality. He is a tree without leaves.

"Do you remember him giving you a bath?"

"No, I don't think so. But he could have. He took care of me when Mother went out. He lived with us until he was killed in an automobile accident when I was four."

"And you think something happened in that bathtub that is causing you pain today?"

"Yes, I do. When I awaken from the dream I have the same fearful prodding I would have if I recalled an unwanted sexual experience."

"But you don't remember being molested?"

"No, I don't. But I was, I'm sure of it. And I have studied enough psychology to know that you have to find the cause before you can find the cure."

"Of course, you are right, Carla. And we will do what we can to find the cause."

Dr. Bianca talks to me and questions me and plans hypnosis for the next session, having decided I am a suitable subject for the procedure.

During the week before my appointment I am fretful yet hopeful that something will surface that I can deal with. Find me the enemy so that I may take aim.

When I meet with her, she asks me to sit in a comfortable chair, then she repeats words that relax me. I feel the tension letting go like the slow release of a rubber band, and succumb to the subtlety of the hypnotic state. Then I am awake.

"Sorry to say, we've run into a dead end, Carla. If you have any repressed memories, we were unable to unearth them. We have made the coffee, but it will not brew."

My heart sinks with the disappointing news. "What do you mean?"

"Only that we couldn't get to them. You remembered Uncle Robbie giving you a bath ..."

"I did?"

"Yes, but nothing more."

"But he did give me a bath?" I find this more encouraging than Dr. Bianca does. "So I've not pulled an incident out of thin air that never happened."

"That's right."

"But why would I remember something as ordinary as a bath unless something important happened there?"

"I don't know, Carla."

"And why would it torment me if it weren't something evil?"

"I just don't know. Believe me, I, too, suspect. But we have no proof."

I leave Dr. Bianca's office more discouraged than when I first saw her. I turn on the motor of the car and drive trancelike through town. The air conditioning isn't working properly, and the South Texas heat rises from the pavement and envelops me.

One should never operate a vehicle in a depressed state of mind. How long have I been driving without knowing where I am? I am unfamiliar with this part of town. This is where colonias have built up, where many illegal immigrants are living. I find myself driving past small trailers and houses that are rundown, all of them in need of a coat of paint. The yards are a nasty mix of dirt and weeds. The streets—Acacia, Esperanza, Bogambilia—slip by. Where am I? I must retrace my path ... regroup ... become alert.

I pull into the gravel driveway of one of the houses to turn the car around, and see a rusty plaque on the door: ALMA BOCANEGRA, CURANDERA, PSÍQUICA.

I am familiar enough with Spanish to know that Alma Bocanegra is a healer and psychic. Had someone or something guided me here? I feel the golden aura of coincidence. I look at my watch. A couple of hours before I must be at work. What harm could it do?

I knock at the door. Alma Bocanegra opens it. She is a Hispanic woman perhaps in her fifties, heavy set, and wearing a long, colorful dress and cheap, bangly jewelry. I introduce myself as Mrs. Benson. I tell her I need help. She understands English.

She ushers me in. The walls of the living room are filled with shelves holding candles, statues and jars, all unfamiliar to me. After all, I tell myself, she is a curandera, a psíquica. She asks me to sit down at a table, brings out candles and lights them. She takes a seat across from me and asks me to talk about myself. "Give me some background, then tell me what kind of help you need." She speaks excellent English with only a faint trace of a Spanish accent.

Briefly I relate the problems of being a single mother and how my marriage solved them. I tell her about the love I feel for my daughter and my husband. That at this time of my life I should be happy instead of bogged down in a jungle of undefined fear. I tell her that this fear is causing serious depression that is hurting my job performance and my family relationship. I have to get to the bottom of it so I can get on with my life.

"And what is generating this fear?" she asks.

"A dream. An innocent enough dream where a man is giving a little girl a bath."

"You suspect something?"

"Yes. I think this man has sexually abused me, but I can't remember. Yet I know I have the answer inside me."

Alma Bocanegra tells me to focus my mind on the dream. "Be perfectly still," she says. She takes hold of my hands. She closes her eyes and asks me to do the same. We sit in heavy silence for several minutes. Then I feel a fullness developing inside me.

Alma Bocanegra's speech is slow and moving. "I am coming into your dream. There is a bathroom. I can see it. Pink tiled walls. A blonde little girl is waist deep in water. There is a man kneeling beside the tub." She pauses as if she is waiting for something.

In the silence I feel my fear, like a hibernating animal, being nudged alert.

She continues. "He is wearing jeans and ..."

I wait for her to say "boots."

"And he is ... he is ..."

I open my eyes and see that hers are as wild as the animal she has teased. I break the silence. "You have seen it, haven't you?"

"Yes, I have seen it. You are right. There is fondling going on."

"Fondling? Nothing more?"

"That is all I see at the moment. But the fondling is inappropriate. A preliminary. There could be more."

"Please. Please try. Tell me what he looks like."

"Not now. I do not see him clearly yet. I need time to ponder. Come again on Friday. Let me keep something of yours. Something personal. I will focus my thoughts on the item and the dream." I remove the necklace I am wearing.

I leave Alma Bocanegra's with ambivalent feelings, excited by her recollections, yet aware that she has said nothing to dispel the notion that she is very possibly a fraud. After all, it was I who conveniently handed her the dream to decorate any way she chose.

I go to work at the hospital, but late in the evening I am unable to concentrate. I ask my supervisor for permission to leave early.

When I return home, Barry and Jennifer sit on the sofa reading a book. They wear matching T-shirts. Jennifer's is large enough to reach her knees. For a moment I am filled with love and gratitude for my family. Some day I will be able to tell them about my illness, and they will understand.

They are surprised to see me. "Carla, aren't you working?" asks Barry.

"No, I had a headache and took off early."

"You've been having headaches a lot lately. Maybe you should see a doctor."

"Yes, I know. But ... I'm feeling better now. Can I join you?" Jennifer scoots herself over to make room for me, and Barry reads a story while the two of us listen.

"I'll give you a break, Barry. Let me get her ready for bed."

Giving Jennifer a bath, I am again reminded of the dream, and purposely do not use bubbles. When she asks for them, I let her have her way, not knowing a reasonable cause for refusal.

When I put her to bed, I smooth her hair and kiss her. She is so much my child—the same smile, the same nose, the same fair complexion. I am determined to get well so that I may again become an important part of her life.

On Friday afternoon I find my way to Alma Bocanegra's home. The psychic repeats the procedure, lighting candles, sitting across from me at the table, taking my hands, asking me to focus on the bath and requesting silence. Again I feel the fullness of something ... or someone ... entering my psyche.

She speaks in a soothing voice. "I am coming into the dream. A bathroom. Pink tiled walls. A little girl with blonde hair. A man is bathing her ... a man whom the little girl trusts. His hands are in the water below the bubbles. He is telling her not to be afraid. But he is hurting her, and she is confused. She starts to cry. He withdraws his hands and strokes her hair, telling her this is what daddies do when they love their little girls ..."

My hands jerk away from Alma Bocanegra's. She is a fraud. I know that now. My father left when I was two years old. It was Uncle Robbie, not my father!

Alma Bocanegra opens her eyes. "I must have said something to startle you."

"You are a fraud," I say.

"I'm sorry, my dear, I saw and heard it. It is true."

I shake my head. I want to get out of here. Alma Bocanegra is not psychic. She is preying on the vulnerable, exploiting them for money. Her intuitive analysis is nothing but the facts I gave her which she then used to develop assumptions.

"It is true, my dear."

I rise from the chair. "I'm leaving now." Bitterly I add, "How much do I owe you?"

Alma Bocanegra's voice is stilted. "You owe me nothing, Jennifer."

Jennifer. She called me Jennifer. Slipping back into my chair, I say, "Why did you call me Jennifer?"

She is confused. "Isn't that your name?"

"No, my name is Carla."

"Who, then, is Jennifer?"

"My daughter is Jennifer."

For several moments we only stare at each other; then she takes my hands. "It is your daughter you are dreaming about and not yourself."

"No. In the dream it is I ... and Uncle Robbie."

"Did you see the two of you clearly?"

"No ... no, I didn't. But ... how could I see Jennifer and ... and ..." My voice is muddled with confusion.

"Because, my dear, you, too, have psychic powers. It has been a difficult revelation for you, but it is a revelation."

"You mean I sensed this was happening." It is not a question. Somehow I know we have found the truth.

"Yes, but you didn't want to see it. You were afraid. Afraid of breaking up your family. So you ran away from it, and that generated more fear and anxiety and pushed the suspicion deep into your mind. But your inner self would not let you get away with the denial."

"If this is true, then what can I do?"

"Go home. It is possible to undo the harm that has been done to Jennifer, but it will not be possible later. And be assured, that when you face the truth, your dreams will cease."

We both stand, and Alma Bocanegra opens her arms, puts them around me and lets my head rest on her shoulder. "You are going to be all right. So is Jennifer."

I murmur "Curandera ... healer."

When I return home, my daughter is still in school and Barry at work. My mind is as clear as a washed chalkboard. The dragons are gone. I have suffered Jennifer's agony, and it is over. I trusted Alma Bocanegra when she told me the damage was repairable. Now that I have exposed the dream and uncovered the enemy, I know I have the ability to tend the wounded spirit of my child.

I cannot mourn the loss of family, since it was only an illusion I conjured from my hopes. I walk to the closet and start removing Barry's clothes.

IRVING

by Eunice Greenhaus

The cut-glass bowl rose from the top of the refrigerator. It turned over in the air and smashed to smithereens on the kitchen floor while we sat at the table and watched, open-mouthed. "What was that!" my husband exclaimed. "It must have been a supersonic jet." replied son Number One. "No, I didn't hear anything." disagreed Number Two. "Neither did I," said Number Three. "It was a ghost," explained Number Four. "Oy Vay," I groaned. Our family had met our resident poltergeist. It would not be our last encounter with him.

Naturally he didn't tell us his name. We decided to give him one. "How about Oy Vay?" suggested my husband "That's what you always say when he does something." "What about Oy Vaying?" one of the boys proposed. No, we agreed, that was too awkward a name. "Oiving" someone said. No, that was too Brooklynese. We changed it to Irving and unanimously agreed that would be his name.

We decided to renovate our house and bought eight windows on sale to replace the old ones. My husband made a wooden rack to hold the glass safely until we were ready to use them. He slipped them into the rack one next to the other and stored them in the back shed. When the day came to put the windows in place my husband went to get them. He came back to the house in a hurry. "Come to the shed," he said, "You have to see this." Curious, we all returned to the shed with him. The three windows at each end of the rack were in perfect shape. The two windows in the middle each had a hole through the center as though they had been kicked in. "Real neat" was the boys' reaction. Irving had been at work again. Oy Vay!

Irving settled in over the years. He never again was as destructive. He had caught our attention! Once I hung a picture over the living room couch. Irving took a dislike to it. That night the picture was on the floor. I hung it back up with a stronger hook. Again it went down. I put it up with a molly screw. I liked that picture! In the morning the picture was on the floor behind the couch. I gave up and put something else in its place. Irving was satisfied and never again bothered it.

Irving began to branch out into things we'd just laid down. As soon as our backs were turned he took them. We searched from attic to cellar looking for the lost item. All of a sudden it appeared just where we put in the first place. He delighted in taking my glasses and probably laughed as I went groping blindly for them. Sometimes Irving kept things for days or even weeks. A favorite pair of shoes would disappear and then come back one day next to the bed.

Several years ago Irving took the remote control to our color TV. We couldn't find it and decided that it had somehow been accidentally thrown out. We finally ordered a new one. We retired, gave our house to our son and his family and moved to the Rio Grande Valley. One day our daughter-in-law called. She was all excited. She had come home from work and "Mom," she screeched "the remote from your old TV is in the middle of my kitchen table." Irving had finally returned it. Unfortunately it was no longer of any use to us since the TV was long gone.

Irving followed us to our new home in the valley. The broiler tray to the new stove vanished without a trace. I broiled a steak for dinner one night. We ate, I washed the dishes and went to get the tray. It wasn't there! No amount of pleading with Irving has ever brought it back. I do hope when he eventually returns it that it's clean.

I've grown old but Irving's kept all his youthful energy. He's not happy that I'm telling his story. The other night he knocked all my notes and pictures off the refrigerator door, scattering them all across the kitchen floor. He broke the magnetic clips that held them into little pieces. Last night he opened the cabinet door under my sink The cat got in there and tore the duct tape off the pipes. Who knows what else he'll be up to if I keep writing!

THE HOUSE THAT ELROD BUILT

by Nina Romberg

"Thanks for buying my little love nest."

Bright blue eyes glowed like marbles rubbed too long between worried fingers. Elrod held out a single small key.

I clutched the key as I watched him walk away. I felt more alone than ever, wanting the feeling and yet hating it. I watched him drive his battered blue pickup down the *caliche* road. Only when my chest hurt did I realize I was holding my breath.

Dragging in air, I inhaled the dust that marked his passage out of my life. I turned my back on him and faced my impulse buy. Unique by any architect's standard but with the power of one man's retirement obsession, the structure was my new home.

His everything was now my everything.

We were both on the rebound, bonded by pain and loss, with one big difference. He faced the end of life while I faced the beginning. I envied him that quicker exit from the pain of our hearts. He'd lost his long-time wife. I'd lost my short-time husband.

Yet we were both moving on with our lives, one stagger step forward, sometimes two back. People safe and secure in their neat little offices had popped in and out of our lives as we reached agreements, signed papers, and finally closed on the house that Elrod built. Suddenly those people were gone. And now the builder as well.

Yes, we promised to stay in touch, but he was one of the Great Generation who valued his privacy and independence. Wyoming was cold enough and far away enough from the sun-kissed Rio Grande Valley of Texas to leave his haunting memories behind, or so he hoped. My memories I left in the concrete canyons of Manhattan, or so I hoped.

We both clung to the belief that distance would hold our memories at bay … and life could begin again.

I approached the house with caution. Do our desires ever truly come true? And if so, what do we do with the reality? I wanted to run and hide, but I'd made the commitment, not only to myself but to my lost love. Raymond had believed in me, but could I believe in myself?

The key looked too small for such a large, multi-level house, and it didn't fit the front door lock. I walked around to the back of the house, a growing fear that I might need to break a window to get inside. What had he said about using the key?

Elrod was small in stature although big in heart and vision. A Hobbit key for a Hobbit house, but now a giant was moving in. At six feet tall, I required a little more head room than most people and I knew I'd need to watch not to bump my head going up and down the stairs inside.

No, the key didn't fit the back door into the garage either. My panic grew. What had he said? The sliding glass doors didn't yield. I looked at the garage doors, then back at the key. Surely the way inside was not through the single garage? I tried the key. It turned and I swung the door upward.

I walked into the area where he had created his masterpiece of a house. The room still vibrated with creativity. Perfect inspiration for me. A deep sink, shelves, and a long cabinet revealed the scars of rough years of work. And there, just as he'd said, were the keys to the house and outbuildings, all neatly identified on small white labels attached to the keys by short white strings. I hated to disturb them. I passed over "no clue" and selected "house."

Feeling a lot like Goldilocks in "The Three Bears," I unlocked the door out of the garage/workroom, stepped onto the terracotta tile of the breezeway/sun room, and after several tries unlocked the door into the house.

Inside, I was assailed by the sights and scents of another person's life, or what was left of it. Elrod had rid himself of most of life's accumulation and sold me the rest. He left me with a sofa and three recliners, no TV. He took that with him.

Upstairs, I knew I'd find three bedrooms and three beds all made up with sheets and bedspreads. Ready to go.

* * * *

I awoke at midnight, the witching hour. Chills raced up and down my body. What woke me? Houses tend to creak and groan in the night, but I heard nothing.

Maybe I should've accepted the shotgun Elrod thought I needed for protection. But what did I know about firearms? I trusted one of his escape hatches better. Maybe he knew more than he shared. After all, how many people build in a door with a ladder leading down into the garage from one bedroom, construct a concrete panic room in the basement, and nail all the windows on the ground floor shut.

I got up and turned on the overhead light, no lamps left for me. I heard nothing, saw nothing, and nothing was getting me out of the locked bedroom.

After dozing fitfully most of the night, I awoke and saw her. At least, I thought I saw a woman sitting in the rocking chair by the window. She looked almost as radiant as the early morning sunlight slanting into the room through gauzy white drapes. She wore blue and almost disappeared into the blueness of the room. She sat with her hands clasped as if in prayer.

My heart thudded in my chest. Visions of ax murderers swam in my head as I reached for the phone beside my bed. Angelic intruder or not, I was calling for help.

"Cara Mia" played throughout the house as the door bell chimed below. I hoped the possible outside threat would distract my intruder. I dropped the phone, leaped from the bed, unlocked the door, and raced downstairs, glad I was wearing comfortable and concealing PJs.

I tried to throw open the door, but first I had to pull out the deadbolt embedded in the floor, fumble open two locks, and then I almost knocked over somebody standing too close to the door.

"There's a woman in my bedroom!" I panted as I looked upward. No silhouette at the window. Had I imagined her or had she escaped through some underground tunnel that Elrod constructed to connect to a storm cellar or something?

"I wish I could say the same," the man with a husky voice said.

"I mean, she's a stranger."

He looked concerned. "I'm James Talbot." He pointed toward a white house down the road. "I'm your nearest neighbor." He hesitated. "You want me to check out your house?"

"Yes, please. I'm Kellie McDermott." Elrod had mentioned that the Talbots lived nearby, so I shook his hand in relief.

As I looked James over, I hoped that I wasn't exchanging one danger for another. Sandy hair cut short, his blue eyes crinkled at the corners from laughter or fatigue. He was about my height, maybe a little older, wearing faded jeans and a blue pullover. I was starting to hate that color. Over all, he appeared the worse for wear. He looked about the way I felt.

He walked back to his truck, pulled something from under the driver's seat, then came back carrying a mean-looking pistol pointed down at his side.

"You're the new owner of the Blue Lady, right?"

"Owner of what?" I tried not to stare at the gun.

"That's what Elrod called his place."

"I didn't know he named it, but he said his wife loved the color blue."

"I guess." He gave a sloppy salute. "Let me check out the place for you."

"You want me to go with you?"

"Make my job easy. Stay here."

*   *   *   *

I sat in the wooden swing hanging from the ceiling of the enclosed breezeway, feeling safer again. I nursed a cup of coffee as I watched James in the blue easy chair across from me.

"Elrod was so devoted to his wife." I gestured around the area. "He built all this for her, and lots of protection to keep her safe. Was she so very beautiful?"

"I never saw her."

"But you're the closest neighbor."

"My parents lived here most of their lives. They're retired now and seeing the USA in their RV. They'd know better than me. I've been gone. Iraq."

Now I understood his look, a man haunted by ghosts and unimaginable horror.

"When you talk to your parents, would you ask them about her?"

"Sure." He set aside his mug and stood up. "Thanks for the coffee."

"Thanks for checking my house." I stood too.

"Look, I know a lot about how the mind and emotions can play tricks." He shook his head as if to dislodge cobwebs. "You got a good deal on this place."

"I wonder why nobody in the area bought it."

"Smart or stupid, who knows? It's yours now so enjoy the beauty, peace and quiet."

I followed him outside. "You enjoy the same."

"Maybe the beauty of the Valley can cure the ugliness I carry inside."

Before I could offer some token peace of mind, he was inside his truck and gone.

And I had to wonder if being alone was such a good idea after all.

*   *   *   *

Time passed in a blur. I no longer slept in the blue bedroom with the adjoining blue bath. A sleeping bag on the cool tile floor of the breezeway did me fine, especially since it joined the garage/studio where I was back to creating the miniature fantastic creatures in clay that had won me money and acclaim worldwide.

Raymond would be proud of me, and I was a little proud of myself. I was back to work. I no longer let his death in that freak car accident obsess me. The fact that everything came out blue was beside the point, and I was even growing fond of the color. Not enough to sleep in the blue bedroom or bathe in the blue bathtub, but enough to create in the many fascinating shades of blue.

James stopped by from time to time, mainly after midnight when we both roamed the night. I paced when I created and sometimes he joined me on my nocturnal wanderings.

On one such night, he turned to me. "I talked with my parents today."

"Where are they?"

"Arizona."

"South or north?"

"North. They get enough of the sun here."

"I felt cold for so long that I want only the soothing heat of the Valley."

"I asked about Elrod's wife."

"She must have been petite."

"I don't know. They don't know. Nobody does."

"I don't understand."

"No one ever saw her."

"Was she sick, maybe bedridden?"

"Maybe he kept her chained in the basement."

"That's not funny. He was devoted to her."

"So you say." James rubbed his chin. "People do things you wouldn't believe under stress and in conflict. Some people do it for fun, others out of duty. Either way, the end result isn't pretty."

"That's war."

"That's people."

"He loved his wife."

"Nobody ever saw her."

"So she was bedridden and he nursed her."

"Maybe she never existed."

"He built all this for her."

"Maybe the Blue Lady is his final tribute to her."

"You think she died before he came here?"

"I don't know. I'm just saying—"

"I don't want to hear it. He loved her. He stayed with her until she died."

"Either way, it doesn't matter. You're here now."

"It does matter. I don't want to live a lie. I want to believe that perfect love for a lifetime is possible. I need to know it."

* * * *

James stayed away a while, but he came back. We didn't talk about the Blue Lady. Instead we helped each other heal, learning to trust another person again. No romance but a commitment. Others were gone from our lives, but we were there for each other.

One day in early September Elrod's blue pickup came sputtering into the front yard, and then the engine coughed several times and died.

I hurried outside from the breezeway and was shocked to see a radically transformed man. He staggered toward me, as if in great pain.

"Kellie, I hate to do this to you, but will you let me die here at the Blue Lady?"

"Die? Here?" I felt frozen to the ground. "I don't understand. I never met a stronger eighty-year-old."

"I thought I could do it." He ran a gnarled hand through his thick white hair. "I thought I could start over."

"What happened?"

"I got the cancer eating me up inside. I won't bother you long."

"No!"

"Are you turning me away?"

"No. I mean, you can't die, not now, not so fast."

"My time's come. I'm ready. I don't want to ever leave the Blue Lady again."

"You don't have to, but I don't want to lose you."

He smiled, just a little tick of one corner of his mouth. "You won't, not so long as you keep watch over the Blue Lady."

"What do you mean?"

"Can I rest in the blue room?"

"Yes, of course." I didn't tell him that I'd never been able to sleep there. "It's all made up and ready."

"Will you bring my bag up? I've only the one. The pickup you might as well have towed to the dump. She'll never run again."

* * * *

That night I met James on the road between our houses, a horrible dread growing in me.

"Elrod won't let me take him to the hospital or even a clinic. Harlingen's not that far away. I think I'll see if I can get a doctor to come out here."

"It looks to me like he came home to die."

"Don't be ghoulish."

"I'd rather bite the dust here than in Iraq."

"When do you go back?"

"Soon."

"I don't know if I can stand any more death around me."

"We need you strong, Kellie. Men always need their women strong."

"I'm not your woman."

"You're my friend. I could sure use some letters and packages from home when I get back over there."

"Maybe I'll sculpt some fantastic little military figures to cheer you up."

"That's my girl." He stepped closer. "And maybe when I get back, you'll be more than my friend."

* * * *

A few days later, Elrod clutched my hand in his feeble one. "Kellie, I've been holding out on you."

"I don't care. I just want you to hold on to life."

"You remember your history lessons?"

"No. And I don't want to."

"Remember the War Between the States?"

"That's the Civil War up north."

"Right. There's an old grave on the east side of the property from that time period."

"I didn't know that."

"It's in a grove of mesquite."

"No wonder I never saw it."

"I want you to bury me there beside that grave."

"No. I don't even think it's legal."

"Kellie, promise me. It's my dying wish. Find a way to bury me there. I entrusted the Blue Lady to you and now I'm entrusting my soul to you."

"Please don't ask me."

"I am. Men depend on their strong women." His voice grew weak with the effort of trying to persuade me.

"I've heard that before, and it won't sway me"

"It's true. I know you'll find a way. My love depends on it. Now let me find a little peace."

I sat there, held his hand, and watched as his bright blue eyes faded away to a still gray. And I let the tears come, once more.

* * * *

James found a way, and on a clear blue morning we stood together in front of two graves, side by side, similar in color, stone, and words.

I read aloud,

<u>MARGARETE. 7 November 1886. My love, I await.</u>
<u>ELROD. 7 November 2006. My love, I return.</u>

WHO

by Eunice Greenhaus

Sounds echo down the empty hall
Ghostly voices seem to call
Frightened I cry: Who are you?
The answer comes back: Who, Who, Who

Into the room I silently creep
Who is there? I begin to weep
My knees start to shake, my voice does too
The answer comes back: Who, Who, Who

A mirror behind me falls with a crash
I turn around and see in a flash
The owl spread his wings, and away he flew
The answer echoes back: Who, Who, Who

A BRUJA'S BENEDICTION

by Bidgie Weber

"Kerchunk. Kerchunk".

The old woman sits on a half-broken rocker on the wraparound porch. The noise as she rocks doesn't bother her. She is part of the rhythm she alone feels.

Today it's just an old rundown white shiplap farm house that stands alone surrounded by Johnson grass, goat heads, sand hills and memories. The once beautiful old house will soon belong to her.

Willacy County in South Texas is hot. The old lady is oblivious to the heat even though she is dressed in a long-sleeved cotton dress long enough to drag in the sand. A heavy shawl is draped over her shoulders. There is no humming noise from an air conditioner. There is no rotating fan to move the hot air. There are only the heat waves bouncing off the tin roof of the house and the "kerchunk kerchunk" of the rocker.

Taunta Val, as she is known in the small farming town of Lyford, feels nothing of this world. She spends most of her waking hours in a place far from the everyday world of farmers and ranchers. When she opens the doors in her mind, Taunta Val steps into the nether world inhabited by ghostly beings and strange voices of people she recognizes by their smoky grey shadows and haunting voices. They bring messages from "the other side".

As frightening as this sounds to you and me, it is a comfort to Taunta Val. She is as at home in this special place as you or I would be in the Lyford café or the

Quick Stop just across the interstate highway a few miles from her place. The old house is not of Taunta's choosing; she was summoned by restless spirits who have messages for their loved ones left behind with their passing.

"Kerchunk. Kerchunk".

Taunta Val slowly rocks back and forth, closes her eyes, and opens the door in her mind. As soon as the way is clear, a dozen voices make themselves heard. Knowing that she must be able to understand each and every word, she gathers her strength and calms the crowd of spirits and ghosts.

This is nothing new for the old woman. Taunta Val is a *bruja*. The daughter of one of old Mexico's most powerful *curanderos* she has abilities most people never imagine exist. For those of you who are unfamiliar with the term, a *bruja* is a witch with the ability to contact people who have traveled beyond the realm of our earthly existence.

For the most part a *bruja* is a messenger. She is summoned when a lost soul or earthbound spirit is unable to complete its journey home. A blessing to her and a curse to some, she sees the future. She is able to guide souls on their way.

Taunta Val has been summoned by restless spirits with messages they have been unable to deliver. She knows there is a vast difference in "dead time" and "living time" which makes it difficult to know how long these spirits have been trying to find a messenger. She has answered the summons and all will be well.

"Kerchunk. Kerchunk".

She relaxes, focuses her "third eye" out across time and space and prepares for whatever comes. Slowly a grayish mist begins to form. The shape appears almost solid. Taunta Val determines the spirit, quickly becoming a ghost, to be a beautiful lady in her late fifties or early sixties. Her red and white gingham dress might have been, at one time, a town dress. Her blue eyes, once as clear as a fresh water lake are clouded by a sadness that peers out from her delicately angled face. The voice Taunta Val hears is a voice of sorrow tinged with anguish.

Taunta Val reaches out to the lady by laying her mind completely open for the message to come. So sad are the sounds that come from the spirit they almost make her heart hurt.

"I have summoned you for this reason; you will deliver a message to my granddaughter thus freeing me to ascend to the paradise that was promised to me at the time of my death."

"Kerchunk. Kerchunk."

Taunta Val continues her rocking and prepares herself to accept the story that follows.

"I left this earth in 1954 and was laid to rest in Restlawn Cemetery here in Lyford Texas. I have been waiting, through no fault of my own, to be on my way but somehow I can't seem to leave this plane. There is someone who will not let me find my way. False feelings of guilt are keeping me earthbound. It is not my sadness that holds me, it is my granddaughter, Leigh, who is responsible. You will be able to learn the secret that holds me hostage in a world where I no longer belong. You can grant us both peace."

As she has so many times before, Taunta Val prepares herself to hear and feel the weight of a story so terrible it keeps this soul trapped in the "between" world and another living a tormented life on earth.

"The day my life's chapter closed was a terrible day in the lives of loved ones left with only memories of me. The one who suffered most was my granddaughter, Leigh. At fifteen Leigh was the light of my life and the family jokester. Mischief and mild mayhem were the order of each day. I know it is she who holds me. I have summoned you to help us both."

At last Taunta Val knows what draws her to the old farm house. Secrets and a task that would sap a normal person's sanity is but another job to a *bruja*.

"Kerchunk. Kerchunk."

The hot Texas sun slowly relinquishes its hold on the day and allows nature to heal the earth of the drying heat of another day. Taunta Val rocks and restores her inner strength that has been drained. She knows exactly who she is to contact and where she is and when she will arrive. Such are the ways of a *bruja*.

Weary old eyes glance up the dirt road where a cloud of dust grows larger and nearer. She hears the roar of a motor. The large black Lincoln pulls up in her drive and the door opens. Halting steps bring a well-dressed woman to the old rocker. She stops and stands face to face with another world. The time has come.

"Do you have the house payment ready for me?"

"Sit and visit for a while, my child. I have more than your house payment for you."

"I have no time to waste dawdling. This place no longer belongs to me and I find it has an unsettling affect on me." "And well it should dear. There are unsettled issues here for you to face. You grew up in this house did you not?"

"The happiest days of my life were spent under this roof. The orange grove, the gardens, the mulberry trees that shaded the entire yard, the pastures, the cotton fields and the seed binds were the only world I knew for fourteen years. How did you know I grew up here?"

"Oh child, I know that and much more. I know of the burden that has been your constant companion since your childhood. I know the people who occupied your young world. I see them often and we talk. I know there is a secret you have kept to yourself for more than forty years. The damage this secret has done is impossible for you to understand. It is within your power to repair this damage and rid yourself of this burden."

Straight forwardness, unfamiliar to the lady, causes her body language to convey a most unfriendly message to Taunta Val. This body language causes no pause for her. As a *bruja* she just smiles at Leigh's attitude.

"I have talked to your grandmother."

"How can you say that? She has been dead since 1954!"

"Her soul has never left this house. She is bound to an existence in neither heaven nor earth. You have tied her to this void by your guilt, by a secret that can release her when revealed."

"I am a bruja who has been summoned by your grandmother in hopes of helping you both. She is a beautiful, sad lonely lady and longs to be on her heavenly way. You know the key and only you can unlock her unhappy existence. Tell me child, what can be of such importance that you have suffered with it since you were fifteen years old?"

The shock to the lady was visible on her face.

"How could you know about that? If you have indeed talked to Big Mommy you are who I also have been searching for. If I tell you what you want to know how will I know that it will make it difference to my grandmother?"

"You will know child, by the words I say."

"I've never told anyone this story. When I was young I used to love to play jokes on people. No one seemed to mind. People always thought my jokes were funny. The jokes were just little things like kids do. One of my favorite jokes was putting a fake fly in someone's soup. No matter how many times I did it the person would always laugh like it was the first time it had ever happened to them."

"I remember the shocking handshake was always good for laughs and surprises. After a while everyone knew what to expect when I held my hand out to shake theirs."

"In the fifties, small farming communities like ours found it difficult to have telephones installed. When our family was able to have a telephone installed it became my special toy."

"One day I made a call to Big Mommy that backfired. I told her she was needed in town. I told her I had been hurt and I was crying for her. I didn't think she would not recognize my voice, but she didn't. She slammed the telephone down, grabbed John, my Grandfather, and ran to the truck and raced to town. By the time they got to our house they looked awful. They were white as a sheet and I thought they would faint right there in our front yard. Of course I had to tell mom and dad what I had done. The 'funny joke' I played wasn't funny at all. I saw how scared Big Mommy and John were and I just stood there crying and telling them how sorry I was. It was just a joke. That was the end of my joking days."

"A year passed. On May the first, nineteen hundred and fifty four my grandmother, the most important person in my life died. The day Big Mommy died my mother told me I was the reason she had a fatal heart attack. If not for the practicable joke that shocked her so badly and weakened her heart she would not have had the deadly heart attack."

"I have never forgotten the fact that I am the cause of Big Mommy's death. Now I find I am still causing her pain and unhappiness. Guilt has been my unwelcome guest for all these years."

"Kerchunk. Kerchunk."

The rocker that has been slowly rocking back and forth slows to a stop. Taunta Val smiles into the eyes of the young woman in front of her.

"Such a small secret to have caused so much pain for so long. A mother whose hurt must have been more than she could bear lashed out with angry words that scared a young girl for life. The desire for forgiveness has held an unhappy soul earthbound for these many years. It is time to turn loose of underserved guilt. Make peace and free your grandmother's spirit."

"Can you do this for me?"

"Child, look into my eyes and tell me what you see."

Looking deep into the *bruja's* eyes, the young woman sees grey shadows forming faces from her past. People she has known and loved. She saw the work-worn face of an old farm hand who lived on the farm when she was a child. She saw her father's face glowing with happiness, her mother's, grandfather's and above them all was her grandmother's face shining with a look of such understanding and forgiveness it made her heart sing.

The old *bruja* explained how she had invited the grandmother to join her to hear the young lady speak.

"Your beloved grandmother was called home when she had a heart attack. You had nothing to do with it. She was called on that day in May so many years ago and she was on her way in the blink of an eye. Let her complete her soul's journey and let yourself complete your life's journey. Worry no more. The torment is over. You both are free."

Just as the *bruja* had promised, having said so, it was so.

"Kerchunk. Kerchunk."

Taunta Val once again leans back and lets the soothing rhythm of the old rocking chair calm her inner being. This was a good day. Good things have been done today.

Only minutes pass before the grey shadow begins to appear. The door remains open and the *bruja* is once again in the company of a netherworld occupant. Something is wrong. Something is making her heart race. Evil is entering. The stench of evil is so strong it makes the skin on Tanunta Val's body shrink. Suddenly aware of the impending danger, she calls on the strength of her *curandero* ancestors to help close the door. After a short but difficult battle the door is finally closed.

"Kerchunk. Kerchunk".

The door is shut. Taunta Val does not see the dark shadow of a foot with sharp claws as it manages to lodge itself between the door and the wall of the "other world". There is no room in the life of a *bruja* for carelessness. One never knows who is knocking on their door. Good and evil spirits and ghosts battle for a chance to return and one must be ever aware of the danger.

Tired and sleepy, Taunta Val reaches for a cool sip of orchata and prepares to bid good-bye to another day.

"Kerchunk. Kerchunk."

As Taunta Val slips into the calming arms of Morpheus the offending foot edges closer and closer to the unguarded doorway and to freedom.

"Kerchunk. Kerchunk."

All is not well in the world of this *bruja*.

MR. WALKER

by Marianna Nelson

Based on real incidents told by Joan Burnard and Marjorie Andrea.

Ray lay asleep in Room 304 until something woke him. For what seemed like many minutes he lay absolutely still. An ominous feeling crept over him, his stomach became a jumble of knots. His body wouldn't move except for the uncontrollable tremors that claimed it.

A beam of light lit the doorway. The beam started to move slowly and Ray's eyes moved to follow it. He could make out menacing shadows advancing toward him silently but steadily. When the shadows reached him, they formed a chain around his bed. Ray was terrified. He couldn't cry out. He still couldn't move and even if he could, the chain would hold him prisoner.

The tallest figure stepped closer. It leaned over, gripped Ray's arm and hissed in his ear, "Don't try anything, Ray. I'm warning you."

Limp as he was, Ray tried to resist the force, to pull away, but the pressure on his arm didn't let up. He managed to blurt out, "W-w-warning me? Warning me about w-w-what?"

"I'm warning you about Mr. Walker. He's coming to collect."

In a hoarse, shaky whisper Ray said, "Collect? Collect what? I-I-I don't owe anybody anything."

Ray hated confrontations. He wished his bed would swallow him so he wouldn't have to deal with these awful beings.

The shapes started to drift away. Before they reached the door, the tallest one turned around and warned him again, "Don't forget, Ray, Mr. Walker's coming to collect."

Ray screamed.

Nothing is more eerie in the middle of the night than a scream of terror. Two aides grabbed flashlights and started running down the hall. When a second scream came, one of the aides said, "Over here, this room."

They rushed into 304. Out of breath and panting, the first aide asked, "What's the matter, Mr. Andrea?"

In a trembling voice he said, "Did you s-s-see them?"

She flipped on the light over Ray's bed. "See who?" she said.

The second aide bent down and patted Ray on the shoulder. "There's no one to see, no one's here," she reassured him. "Everything's okay, Mr. Andrea."

"No, it isn't!" he said, strength returning to his voice. "They were here, in this very room. I saw them. I heard them. They threatened me. One of them grabbed my arm and held it down."

The first aide checked his arm. Red marks were on his skin. Even though she told him again that he'd be all right, she wasn't so sure herself. Where had those pressure marks come from anyway?

"Those men, they were here," he said. "They said Mr. Walker's coming to get me, Mr. Walker's coming to collect!"

The aides looked at each other. Mr. *Walker*? Both of them were thinking the same thing. Their looks of concern changed to looks of fright. They stepped aside so Ray couldn't see how scared they were.

"Could it be the same Mr. Walker?" the first aide asked. "The one everyone talked about, the one who never had visitors but received lots of mail, more than the other patients? But would *that* Mr. Walker torment another patient?"

Neither aide remembered any more about him except that he'd died. And of course a dead person wouldn't be here now—unless he were a …

The "g" word scared the aides—they didn't want to think about it, let alone say it. Working the night shift had its perils. They knew that visits from the paranormal happened in nursing homes but that didn't make them any less unnerving. The aides wanted to turn their attention back to the real world, back to things they could control.

They talked to Ray and decided to move him to another room. But come sunup, the day staff forgot to notify his wife and stepdaughter that he'd been moved during the night.

Nursing homes are *so* depressing—I'd rather die first.

That thought went through Joan Burnard's head as she turned into Resaca Center's parking lot. She'd come to visit her 90-year-old, 90-pound step-father, Ray Andrea. Her mother Marj would come later but for now Joan was on her own. To fortify herself for the mission ahead, she drank a few swigs of Starbuck's before getting a can of ginger ale from her cooler for Ray.

Joan went into the nursing center and paused at the doorway to sniff the air. Urine. The smell was unmistakable. The odor was always there, even though the facility was clean and the staff of mostly Certified Medical Aides were diligent about keeping patients dry.

Near the entryway six patients sat in wheelchairs, their fingers fidgeting with their clothing, their heads bent over. Looking down at the floor the way they were, they didn't see a bald-headed woman walk confidently by them. If they'd been aware of things around them, they would have been surprised to see a woman in public without the customary wig or head cover that one wears when undergoing chemotherapy.

Staying cool and comfortable was more important to Joan than conforming to custom. Besides, she knew she had a nicely-shaped head. And how did she get that head? Was it because her mother had turned her often in her crib? Or was it just good genes? She didn't know. It boosted her confidence and self-esteem now.

Walking past other patients on her way to the west wing, Joan reached Room 304 where Ray had been moved yesterday. She went in and waited briefly for her eyes to adjust to the dim interior.

"Ray?"

No answer.

"Ray?" she said again, this time a little louder.

Still no answer.

The room was surprisingly quiet, the oxygen machine's soothing hum was missing. She went over to the unmade bed and gingerly touched the covers, patting her hand around a little feeling for the shape of something underneath. The bed was empty. Ray wasn't in his room! Her heart skipped a beat. Oh no, she thought, he's died in the middle of the night and they haven't gotten around to telling mother or me.

Across the hall Peg Anderson sat next to her husband, a place where she spent most of her time lately. Dick had had a stroke and couldn't speak. The blank expression on his face never changed. Peg wasn't sure he even recognized her anymore.

When Peg glanced up from Dick's bedside, she noticed a bald-headed woman walking into Ray's old room. Oh no, she thought, it's Joan. She probably doesn't know what happened.

She went across the hall and put an arm around Joan's shoulder. "Didn't they tell you, dear?"

Joan looked startled. "Tell me *what*?" she said.

"That Ray's been moved, moved to Room 204. I thought I should tell you, in case they forgot."

"Oh, thank God! He's still alive!" Joan exclaimed. "But why did they move him? This is the *fourth* time in almost *three* weeks!"

Peg had expected this question, of course, and knew she would have to tell everything carefully so as not to alarm Joan any more. She began the story by saying, "In the middle of the night something must have woken Ray. He was frightened. The aides were trying to calm him even though they seemed frightened, too." Peg paused. "He told them that a group of men had been in his room, men who warned him that a Mr. Walker was coming to collect. Because he was so distraught, the aides thought it would be better to move him to another room."

"Maybe he just had a bad dream," Joan said. Or, heaven forbid, she thought, maybe it was something else, something worse.

As for the name Walker, Joan didn't think Ray knew any Walkers except his cousin Henry. But he would have called him Henry, not Mr. Walker, and of course Henry wouldn't have done such a thing anyway.

"Do you know anyone named Walker, Peg?"

Peg didn't want Joan to know the rest of the story, but she felt she had to answer her question. "Yes," she said. "Mr. Walker used to be a patient here, but … but he died a while back."

Joan stared unbelievingly at Peg as she told the story. "That's impossible!" Joan said. Her head began to ache with the awfulness of the thing that had happened to Ray—or the thing he *thought* had happened to him. After all, maybe it still was just a bad dream. Please, please, she prayed, let it be a dream.

For now she had to find Ray to see if he was okay. "I really must leave," she told Peg. "I'm sorry if I was abrupt and distracted before, but I've got a lot on my mind right now."

"Don't worry, Joan," Peg said, "I understand."

On the way to the east wing, Joan tried to put this and other things in perspective. She recalled how foggy and distant Ray had seemed the last time mother and she had visited him, before all this Mr. Walker business happened.

He'd said, "Well, I guess it's getting late and Marj isn't coming."

Marj spoke up right away. "What are you talking about, Ray? I'm Marj. Don't you remember me, sweetheart?"

He looked at her blankly.

Then Joan said to Ray, "Do you know who I am?"

He looked at her vaguely and said, "No, not really."

Then she asked again if he knew who Marj was. He looked right at Marj and said, "I don't know." Today was the only time he hadn't recognized her.

Then Ray asked, "Isn't it time for you to leave?" He'd never said that before, he'd always wanted them to stay longer.

* * * *

In the east wing, Joan went to number 204. She waited by the door, heard the familiar sound of an oxygen machine, and peeked in the room. Ray was lying in the bed. She walked over to him, kissed his cheek and smoothed his hair on his forehead. His skin felt cold and he was shaking. As she stroked his arm she noticed red marks on his skin.

"These marks on your arm, Ray, where did they come from?" Joan asked.

He answered in short, breathless bursts. "That man grabbed my arm. It hurt. I tried to get away but couldn't."

"What man?" Joan asked.

"The one who came in the night."

Ray told her he'd gotten sick later, that he couldn't eat and his stomach was upset. She tried to get him to sip some ginger ale, but he pushed it away. He seemed obsessed. "Did those men come back?" he asked. "Are you sure all my bills are paid? Is that insurance thing straightened out?"

"Everything's okay, Ray. Marj is taking care of your bills and the insurance."

Trying to release Ray's mind from his worries, Joan began to bring him back to the real world. "Do you know who I am?" she asked.

"Yes," he said, "you're the bald one."

She smiled. He recognizes me today, she thought, or at least he knows that I'm the one with no hair.

When Marj walked in, Ray recognized his Marj and called her by name. This gave her hope that he might come home again. Yes, no matter what had happened the night before, Ray was back in the real world, at least for now. Even so, Joan felt that the improvement would only be temporary. She didn't see how he could survive the shock of Mr. Walker's threat.

* * * *

The call came at 8 o'clock the next morning. Ray had died. The nurse said he'd been sitting in his wheelchair waiting for breakfast. His chin was down. When the aides went over to check him, he was gone.

For the rest of the morning Marj and Joan consoled each other and made the necessary phone calls. By afternoon Joan was still red-eyed and tired, but she knew she had to go to the nursing home one last time to pick up Ray's belongings.

When she got to Ray's last room, #204, she saw the empty bed all made up with fresh sheets. She looked at their whiteness and knew that even though Ray's body was no longer in the room, his spirit was still in her heart.

The thought comforted her and gave her strength to do what she had to do. She went to the night stand beside the bed. Opening the drawer and the cabinet underneath, she took out clothing she recognized as Ray's. But there was something else. In a plastic hospital basin was an unopened bank statement. She picked up the basin. Under it were more statements. Why hasn't anyone cleaned these out, she wondered. But that wasn't all. Next to the closet was a dresser and inside it was more unopened mail. All the mail was addressed to a Mr. Walker.

"Walker! Oh, my God!" Joan exclaimed. "That's the name of the man who was going to collect from Ray!"

Right away she brought the letters to the nursing office. Alma Banderas, the supervisor in charge, was a pleasant woman a few years older than Joan who was used to dealing with other people's problems. When she saw the puzzled look on Joan's face and the letters in her hand, she knew this would be yet another problem to solve.

Joan explained the strange happening involving Mr. Walker and then handed Alma the letters she'd found in Ray's room. As she looked at the envelopes, there was a flash of recognition on her face. "I remember a Mr. Walker," Alma said. "Funny, but no one seemed to know his first name—his mail just had his initials. He died a while back. It's puzzling, though, why these letters addressed to Mr. Walker were found in Mr. Andrea's room," she said.

"Puzzling?" Joan said.

Pausing a minute to look up the name Walker in the census records on her desk, Alma looked at Joan and said, "Puzzling because Mr. Walker never stayed in 204. He was on another wing. Furthermore, his night stand couldn't possibly have been moved. Furniture is *never* moved from room to room. It's a firm rule that when a patient is transferred, only his bed goes with him."

Well, I'll be darned, Joan thought, Mr. Walker's night stand and dresser had not been moved from another room. This woman had just poked a hole in what would have been a logical explanation to the mystery of the letters.

When their eyes met again, Alma changed the subject. "Now, about what happened to your stepfather. Some things just can't be explained rationally. On the other hand, changes—like finding oneself in a different room—are disturbing to patients who have dementia, even those with just the beginnings of dementia. Who knows what goes through their minds?"

After that, there was really nothing more to say. As Joan left the office Alma looked at the back of Joan and thought, what a nicely-shaped head that woman has. I wonder if her mother turned her often as a baby.

* * * *

On the way home, Joan remembered having read something about a study done in nursing homes. She'd seen it just recently. Where was it? Oh, yes, in *The Lovely Bones*, a novel by Alice Sebold. The study said many patients had seen someone standing by their bed at night, an intruder who often talked to them or called their name. The researcher concluded that these visions were the result of small strokes that often preceded death.

Joan didn't know if this had been a real study—after all, the book was fiction—but it seemed that it could be real. Anyway, it didn't seem to apply to Ray because the men in his room were very real—at least to him. And what about the red marks on his arm—weren't they proof that he'd been grabbed?

The mystery couldn't be solved unless ... unless one believed in ghosts. And, if one did, why wouldn't or why couldn't a ghost come back to get his mail? After all, she'd heard people say that some ghosts come back to earth to take care of their unfinished business. Maybe that was the case with Mr. Walker. But if mail was all Mr. Walker wanted, why did the ghosts torment Ray and cause him such anguish? That's what made her really angry.

Maybe the ghosts had played a practical joke on Ray. If they had—and if she could find them—she'd tell them that what they'd done wasn't at all funny. She could just picture the scene. She'd shake a finger at them and say, "Naughty, naughty ghosts!" She'd scold them and tell them to apologize. They'd act contrite—like little kids when they're caught doing something bad. They'd hang their heads in shame and mumble that they were sorry. Before she finished with them, she'd scold them one more time and then order them to take their mail and go!

Enough of this business about ghosts! It was time to get on with her life. She started thinking about her return to Dallas after Ray's funeral. She would get her last round of chemotherapy. During that ordeal she and mother would be there for each other with frequent phone calls and occasional visits. Mother was strong and resilient and would survive, just as Joan knew she would too.

MYTHICAL MAGIC VALLEY

by Nelly Venselaar

The breezy, blowy, blustering nor'eastern hits the shore.
Banks and beaches are braced and
Buttressed by boulders and sandbags.
Waves are fantastically high
Dark greenish with dirty beigey fringes
Rolling on top and over each other.
Painting a moody picture
Providing an unforgiving
Perturbing feeling.
Ghostly sailors ride the surf.
A fleet of armed galleons filled with pirates or conquistadors.
Is there a ghost appearing in the mists above the spraying waves?
Could there be a sea-demon living in this rumbling surf
Where pirates and soldiers have gone into their watery graves?
Shadowy apparitions top the waves in the moonlight.
Wave after tumbling wave
Comes down in fury, crashing like thunder above
The sounds like moaning sailors or creaking sunken ships.
Sea foam spray is from up high

Over harbor walls onto the yachts
With a crashing thunderous rumble.
A photographer moves towards the seething sea
Trying to portray a moody picture
Of these fascinating rumbling waves.
A fisherman ploughs against the whistling wind to check his boat in the harbor.
The waves splash at its sides.
No boat is sighted out there in these cruel, merciless waters.
It would be beaten and broken into these waters, dark and deep.
Caught up by atmosphere, seeing the wild, restless ever-changing sea
There is a search for the mysterious and a sense of wonder.
Is that guitar music joining the babbling, rippling Rio?
Trees are creaking, cracking and snapping in this stormy gale.
One heroic seagull tries flying against the fierce boisterous wind.
He is sent back, but with stamina he tries again and again.
This now evil-looking ocean has majestic beauty;
But all are looking forward to the calming of the sea
To enjoy against the appeal and charm of beach and vale.

NIGHT SHIFT

by Janice Workman

High heels clack down the hallway, followed by the "Thump" of the time clock checking in an employee.

"Who's there?" shouts Manuel, hemmed in by the wet floor and his mop bucket.

No answer. His voice resonates in the empty clinic.

"Maria, is that you?" he persists. Wringing out the wet mop, he prepares to swish it down the hall toward the sound. He knows the housekeeper won't stay past 6:00 p.m. even for time-and-a-half, but maybe her ride's running late.

No answer.

Since he started the night shift two weeks ago he always hears the same sound. High heels, time clock, then nothing.

Manuel considers rumors he heard about ghosts in the clinic:

"They say it's just the building settling, and tell me to put out more rat traps," cautioned Jaime, the daytime custodian. "Yeah, right. You're the third person we've hired for the late shift in two months. But we're not supposed to talk about it."

Maria ends her day shift tidying up the rear waiting room. One month ago she found the chairs in a circle not five minutes after she had arranged them in neat rows. "No one else was there," she told Manuel in a hushed voice, eyes wide with remembered fear. "Minnie and I were both in the break room. I tell you, that clock hits 5:30 and I'm outta here!"

He shivers as he enters the sterile stainless environment of the radiology room. It always feels colder here than in the rest of the clinic. Maybe it's all the equipment. Maybe it's what Jaime told him about his predecessor:

"Manny, I swear. Jimbo—the guy that had this job before you; he told me the night he quit he was cleaning the floor by the x-ray machine when he heard a voice come out of the wall." Jaime stopped for a sip of coke, wiped a hand across his face and went on. "Lorena, *ayuda me! Saca me de aquí!*" He paused again, looked around before continuing, "He asked me what it meant. When I told him, 'Lorena, help me! Get me out of here!' That was it for him."

Manuel leaves the chill of the room and its memory behind him. He closes the door to finish his rounds.

A whisper of nylon moving against nylon catches his ear. A scent much more feminine than the disinfectant he uses on the countertops wafts by his nose. He catches a glimpse of long legs and short skirt, a flash of creamy skin and blonde hair. "Hey," he calls, "I'm just about done here. Then I have to lock up."

No answer.

"Rats?" Manuel mutters through gritted teeth as he empties the trash from small baskets into the large wheeled container.

He moves room to room, switching off lights and locking doors. All the offices are empty; the hallways, quiet. He shrugs as he steps out into the humid night and turns the key in the heavy glass front door. A wavering luminescence holds his attention for a moment, but with bills to pay and a baby on the way, he's damned certain it's a trick of the security lights playing off defects in the window.

THE AFTERNOON WALK

by Verne Wheelwright

The afternoon had been very pleasant. Friends from the West Coast were visiting us in Harlingen, and we had taken them to a wildlife refuge on the Rio Grande, not far from our home. The four of us had spent the afternoon walking trails, catching up on old times, and admiring the wildlife. We'd brought binoculars and cameras and had taken lots of pictures of birds, butterflies and each other.

It was a pretty typical early Fall afternoon in the Rio Grande Valley, with temperatures in the mid-nineties, but we had come fairly late in the day, so a breeze from the southeast had come up, carrying cooler air off the river. It was late enough in the day that even though the sun had not quite set, a full moon was already rising, so we all started moving along the trail in the direction of the parking lot.

I lagged a little behind, fascinated by a Green Jay at one of the feeders just off the trail. And I might add, if you don't know what a Green Jay is, take a minute to look up a picture in Google Images, then you'll understand some of my fascination. Anyway, as I watched this bird, my wife and friends walked on, disappearing around a bend in the path, so I started on to catch up, but was again distracted by several hummingbirds, apparently part of the migration already headed south for the winter.

I realized that the sun was starting to set and light was fading, so I resumed my way down the path toward the parking area. I hadn't gone far when I met a lady coming from the other direction. She appeared somehow distressed, and I sensed a feeling of deep sadness. As she approached, I spoke, not really knowing why but I felt she needed help, and I asked "May I help you?"

She kept walking without really looking at me, but I heard her say "Ay, mis hijos!" Although I've lived in the Valley for several years, I still don't speak Spanish very well, but I understood her to say "Oh, my children!" Yet she clearly didn't want my help and she kept walking until she was out of sight behind the tall grasses and the fading light. I walked on down the trail, wondering what I could do. Since she didn't seem to want my help, it certainly didn't make sense to run after her, but what if her children were lost? And it was starting to get dark.

I picked up my pace, hoping to catch up with my wife and friends, also hoping they'd stopped to look at something along the way and weren't standing in the parking lot waiting for me to arrive with the keys to the car! As I neared the end of the path, I saw a park ranger coming; probably checking the trails to be sure everyone was out of the park before darkness. Stopping, I told her about my encounter with the lady who was looking for her children.

The young park ranger hesitated, "Where did you see her?" she asked. "Along this path, near the river. Probably 200 yards or so further on," I answered, pointing in the direction from which I had just come. Again the hesitation. "Was she wearing a white dress?" Realizing the ranger must know the lady I had seen, I smiled and said, "Yes, she was. It was fairly long."

The young park ranger's dark eyes looked troubled and she seemed a little pale. She reached out and took my arm, then started walking with me, slowly, in the direction of the parking lot. "I don't think there is anything we can do to help her this evening," she said gently. I wasn't quite sure what she meant, and asked her. "Your friends are waiting" she said, "so let's talk while we walk, but the fact is, you've just met our resident ghost!"

When I was very young, I heard lots of ghost stories, and was afraid of ghosts because I thought they might harm me. As I grew older, I became less afraid and more curious about the possibility that ghosts might exist, and wondered how I would go about seeing one—but without any risk! As a teen, I read a lot of books about ghosts and other paranormal experiences

By the time I became a grandfather I had become more skeptical. I guessed that ghosts were a possibility, but I felt they were very unlikely to exist. I tried to keep my mind open on the subject, but really gave it very little thought. But, I remembered that when my son had died not too many years ago, I thought that he had spoken to me. Several times. Very clearly. But I attributed that to wishful thinking, because I <u>wanted</u> to hear from him.

So now, I had actually encountered a ghost?

"And what does that mean?" I asked. "Isn't meeting a ghost a warning of impending death or some terrible event?" She smiled, almost laughed, and replied, "Not in this case. Many of us here in the park have met this woman over the years, and we're all doing just fine. No ill effects." Then I asked the obvious question, "Who is she?"

"Well, she's truly a legend that goes back at least a hundred years. There are a lot of different stories about her, but generally they all boil down to a young woman with small children who has been abandoned by her husband. She eventually realized that no other man would take her in, much less marry and support her, and she had no way to feed her babies. Desperate out of her mind, she threw her babies into the river and watched them drown. Grieving and inconsolable, she eventually died of sorrow and starvation. Now she walks the river looking for her babies."

Her description of the plight of the woman I had seen was very sympathetic, with no sense of fear or apprehension, but with an acceptance of the unexplainable as just that—unexplainable. By this time, we had arrived at the parking area, and the young ranger said, "I really enjoyed talking with you, and I hope you won't let any of this worry you," then with a smile and a wave, she returned to her duties.

When I reached the car, my wife jokingly asked, "Did they send the park rangers out to bring your back?" I replied, "Not exactly, but it's a long, interesting story. I'll tell you all about it on the drive home."

I've thought about that day many times since then, and about the two very different young women divided by over a century, yet literally crossing paths in our time. It also made me wonder about incidents over my own lifetime that might have provided opportunities to understand something that I couldn't. And because I couldn't, or wouldn't, understand I missed those opportunities. I won't again.

My encounter has also caused me to wonder if times have changed that much over the centuries, knowing that in recent years several women in the U.S. have gone to jail or mental institutions for drowning their children or killing them in other ways. Sometimes these acts are malicious, simply to get rid of the children, but other times they appear to be acts of desperation to save the children from the lives that they are in. These women have been or are being punished for their crimes, but none will face a fate like that of the woman I met during a late afternoon walk by the river.

About the Authors

The authors of the stories and poems in this book have several things in common: they enjoy writing, they work hard at their craft, and they are all members of the Valley Byliners, a local writing club in Harlingen, Texas. This book is a project that brought all of these writers together, most writing in a different style or manner than they had before.

Each of these writers has created a story, revised it, submitted it for editing, then made more revisions. They have defined and reviewed the logics of their plots, described their settings, introduced and developed their characters and carefully chosen the words that they felt would best convey their stories to you, the reader.

Several of these authors are professionals who write every day while others write less for publication than for the pure pleasure of writing. Some of these writers have retired from other careers and now find that they have discretionary time in which they can write. And they all write with one goal, to create a story that you will enjoy, find interesting or even remember.

All of us who have participated in the creation of this book hope that these stories will achieve that goal for you.

Andersson, C. Dean

C. Dean has never seen a Chupacabra but wants to. He was weird even before writing novels like <u>I Am Dracula</u> and an heroic fantasy trilogy about Bloodsong, a never-say-die warrior woman who's already been dead, a while, when her story begins. Visit <u>www.cdeanandersson.com</u>. Read his books. Be weird yourself. And have fun!

Cate, Robin

Robin has been writing poetry for thirty years and finds the Rio Grande Valley a gorgeous subject for her verse. She is currently working on Pocket-books, small books of poetry that she sells for non-profits and gives to interested readers.

Greenfield, Ann

Ann is a native Texan, born in Austin, raised in Amarillo. She moved to McAllen with her husband in 1982. Ann has two grown boys, and received a BS in Education from Texas State. As a docent for MOSTH, Ann was fascinated by the old jail. *The Hanging Room* is her first published story.

Greenhaus, Eunice

Eunice retired from a supervisory position with the IRS after raising four boys. Eunice, along with her husband and their Doberman, Killa, moved into a 28' trailer in which they spent the next five years touring the country. They finally settled at a San Benito park where she teaches Mah Jongg and writes her memoirs and poems.

Johnson, Marjorie (Marge)

Marge moved to Weslaco in 1957, where she authored publications for the Rio Grande Valley Partnership/Chamber of Commerce) for 37 years. Under its sponsorship she published the <u>Valley Proud History Cookbook</u> (1991) and <u>Historic Rio Grande Valley</u> (2001). Since her 2004 retirement, she does publicity for the Weslaco Museum and other good causes.

Mattei, Eileen

After moving north to Harlingen, Eileen Mattei was seduced by the Valley's natural and cultural assets and became a writer to tell the region's stories. Magazines, books and ad agencies offer outlets for her imagination.

Moreno-Hinojosa, Hernán

Hernán's first major published work was in 1994, Candelaria's Sorrow, a true ghost story. Since then he has had two books published, the first in 2003 by the University of Houston: The Ghostly Rider and Other Chilling Stories and in 2004, The Night the Moon Came Down by the Virtual Bookworm in College Station. He considers the Valley his second home.

Nelson, Marianna

In 1997 Marianna and Bruce Nelson sold their Connecticut home to live in a 26' house on wheels. In 1998 they pulled into San Benito and hopped on a merry-go-round of activities. Marianna tutors kids, leads a writers group, volunteers for KMBH Public Radio/TV, writes Byliners news releases, and composes a photo journal for the Nelson's Web site at www.otr.studio221.net. Also, she plans to compile a book of old photos with stories that she's written about her younger years.

Romberg, Nina

Nina writes dark thrillers and historical romance as Jane Archer. Twenty of her books are in print worldwide. Her first novel was a bestseller with 500,000 copies sold. Out of the West was optioned for a television movie. Stories from The First Fire and Texas Indian Myths and Legends are featured on audio in Abilene's Frontier Texas! See www.ninaromberg.com and/or www.janearcher.com.

Sizer, Mona D.

This former Dallas English teacher is the author of 32 works of fiction, history, biography, and true crime as well as poetry. She grew up in the Valley and lives in Harlingen. She is currently at work on a new book Texans Outrageous.

Stevens, Judy

Judy has been a rockhound, potter, cartoonist, and ecclectic collector. Originally from Minnesota by way of Southern California, she came to the Rio Grande Valley in January 1977 with her husband and daughter. Nowadays, she delights in watching the grandkids grow and in hanging out with the grandpa.

Tuxbury, Georgia

Georgia went back to school after raising five children and worked in public relations where her job entailed writing and public speaking. She began to pursue free-lance writing when her husband retired. Since then she has sold short stories, poetry, plays and is now the South Texas reporter for Southwest Farm Press.

Vela, Sandra

Sandra Vela is a Rio Grande Valley native and descendant of one of the pioneer families of Weslaco. Sandra is the Byliner's newsletter editor, and is currently working on her first novel set in the South titled Women Well Seasoned.

Weber, Bidgie

"Returning to my Valley roots after forty years has been wonderful. A new career, new interests, new friends and writing, a new passion have been the "pot of gold" at the end of my rainbow. My ten year association with the Byliners has allowed me to 'sing my songs.'"

Wheelwright, Verne

Verne and Betty have lived in Harlingen, Texas since 1999, when they moved here from Houston. Verne has written several articles and a workbook describing how individuals can apply futurist's methods to their personal lives. He is now working on a book about personal futures. His web site is www.personalfutures.net

Wilder, Janet R.

Janet found The Valley as an RVer and after eight years made the Rangerville area her permanent home. The former publisher of an RV newsletter and freelance Travel and RV consumer publication journalist, she would like to concentrate on writing fiction.

Workman, Janice

"I've been writing ever since I first put crayon to wallpaper. Life is my inspiration: past, present, future, fiction, fact. I am waiting to be discovered while I work on the next Pulitzer prize winning novel. As a ByLiner member, I am grateful for the group's encouragement and expertise."

Zúñiga Campos, Berta

Berta, a retired public school teacher, lives in Harlingen, Texas with her husband Gene. She has two married daughters and two granddaughters. In 1999, she earned a doctorate in education from the University of Houston. In addition to writing memoir, she enjoys travel and photography. She plans to produce a photo book upon her return from her trip to southern Europe.

978-0-595-42063-6
0-595-42063-X

Printed in the United States
71350LV00004B/1-138